THE SICILIAN'S BETRAYAL

THE DIMARCO EMPIRE

CINDY REDDING

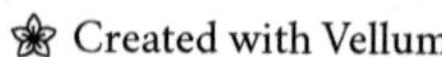 Created with Vellum

*For my husband Michael,
and my beautiful daughters, H & J,
I love you.*

CHAPTER 1

*L*iz handed her client the receipt for the gold watch she'd purchased as a holiday gift.

With a burst of brisk winter air and laughter, a tall and handsome man walked in, with snowflakes sprinkled across the broad shoulders of his topcoat. His black hair glistened with melting snow. The woman on his arm was just as tall, with long, platinum-blond hair. She wore a full-length dark mink coat, the matching hat angled on her head, and on her feet were black high-heeled leather boots. They both carried gift bags from designer boutiques. The boxes peeking out of the bags were wrapped in red and green festive paper, with gold and silver bows, ready for Christmas. They were laughing and enjoying themselves, shopping along Fifth Avenue.

Coming around the long glass counter, Liz gave her client the gift-wrapped package. "Have a Merry Christmas. Please be careful out there. The Weather Channel is predicting a blizzard." She walked with her client to the door where the falling snowflakes dotted the air and melted as they landed on the concrete.

"Thanks, Liz. Have a happy holiday."

Liz turned with a smile to greet the new customers. She took a step back, her heart frozen, the greeting died on her lips. *Rico!* She hoped they didn't notice her stunned expression. The man seemed to be looking through her as he said in his Italian-accented voice, "We wish to see the ruby and diamond necklace you have in the window."

"Ah… Ah… Ye-Yes," she stammered, her voice sounding strange to her own ears. "Please come with me to our private showing salon." Walking in front of them, Liz snapped out of her momentary daze and tried to control the turmoil brewing in her head. Her thoughts were running wild. *It couldn't be him, but this man could be his twin. Only Ricardo doesn't have a twin.*

Taking a breath, she opened the door to the VIP room, allowing the couple to enter. They placed their purchases on the shiny mahogany table. Then the tall, darkly handsome man helped the beautiful woman remove her coat. He gave the mink to Liz, without so much as looking at her. Hanging the fur on a gold-toned hanger, she placed it carefully in the closet. When Liz turned, he was there. She'd nearly walked into him.

He handed her his coat, his fragrance clinging to the cashmere, the fabric still warm from his body. Mumbling an apology, which he ignored, she breathed deep, trying to still her trembling hands. *Big mistake!* The scent of his cologne wafted in the air. Her heart tripped in her chest. Liz stood tall and offered them a beverage, which they both declined. The woman sat in one of the red leather armchairs at the mahogany table, her blond hair flowing around her. The man remained standing, his hand on the back of her chair.

When she was sure they were comfortable, Liz said, "I'll be back with the necklace you wish to see."

Returning with the beautiful one-of-a-kind diamond-and

ruby-necklace, she laid it on a blue velvet display mat. Again, Liz froze. The gorgeous blonde had taken off her leather gloves and on her left hand was a pear-shaped diamond at least five carats; on either side were pear-shaped stones of at least one carat each. Without a doubt, an engagement ring.

The man's eyes bored into Liz. She was beside herself. He looked like Ricardo, he sounded like Ricardo, with that dreamy Italian accent and his deep baritone voice. The voice she still heard in her dreams. Her hands shook as she helped the beautiful blonde hold up the necklace and examine it.

The woman turned to the man. "It's perfect."

He bent to look at the piece, took it from her hand, and examined it more closely. Looking at the necklace and not Liz, he said, "Tell me about the quality, the origin of the stones, the carat weight."

Liz tried so hard not to stare, but she couldn't help it; she was positive it was him. She remembered that Ricardo liked tall blondes, he even had joked that Liz was his first redhead. He'd told her how much he loved the way her hair resembled flames of fire and how much he liked her wearing it down around her shoulders.

Controlling her voice so it didn't quiver, she said, "There are forty-three oval Burma rubies, alternating with forty-three brilliant-cut diamonds." She glanced down at the description card. "The mounting is platinum and eighteen-karat yellow gold."

Finally, the woman turned to Liz. "We will take it. Can you wrap it for us?"

The man pulled out his credit card and looked directly into Liz's eyes as he handed it to her. There in bold letters on the black metal card was his name, Ricardo Antonio DiMarco.

She picked up the necklace. "I will be right back." Her voice was a husky whisper. She went into a side room, so she could wrap the gift and run the black metal credit card. Knowing there would be no problem, the two-hundred-thousand-dollar purchase price would be approved. Liz smirked, thinking he could have bought ten necklaces without issue.

Did he not recognize her? After all they had been to each other? She gently placed the necklace in a red velvet box. Her fingers were too stiff to tie the bow on the package. Trying desperately to snap out of her daze, she managed to make a neat bow with the gold ribbon. Then she placed the box inside a red bag and filled it with gold tissue paper. She brought out the package, along with the receipt that required his signature, and handed him a silver pen.

"Mr. DiMarco, would you please sign the receipt?" She wouldn't look at him.

Even with her hair piled high on her head and her high heels, she barely reached his shoulder. He took the pen and, in his bold handwriting, scribbled his signature. His long, lean fingers brushed against hers as he handed back the receipt, sending a jolt of electricity through her body. She jerked her head up and couldn't help but look at him. Fathomless black eyes burned into her soul. She swallowed and looked away. With a hand that shook, her fingers stiff, she gave him the package.

He took it and gave it to the woman. "Sofia, here, *cara*."

Liz remembered the endearment so well. *Cara* meant darling in Italian. *He used to call me cara.*

Sofia smiled and accepted the package from Ricardo. Liz went to get Sofia's mink. Ricardo followed, taking the coat from her. Liz couldn't help but feel a pang of sorrow as he helped the beautiful woman into the mink coat. She followed with his coat. Ricardo took it and turned, not even acknowledging Liz. Once they were ready, she led the couple out of the room and walked them to the front door.

The two left the jewelry store without saying a word, his hand on the small of Sofia's back. Liz stood there watching as they got into a limousine. He never looked back or said anything else. Perplexed by the chance encounter, she stood there long after the limo pulled away, wishing it had just been a dream.

Liz's heart sank. He'd always called her *cara*. The whole encounter had been so disturbing, she needed to sit down for a moment. Luckily, her co-worker was back from her break, so Liz could take hers. She walked into the employee's break room, her hands still trembling, her body cold. She poured a cup of coffee and sat down, wrapping both hands around the mug to take in the warmth from the cup, the steam rising. She went over what had just happened. *It was him, but he didn't recognize me. Well, that was a blessing. Though how? With all we had been to each other.* She couldn't understand.

A sadness she thought gone crept over her. At one time, he'd loved her and now, here he was engaged to marry another. She had to get out of the jewelry store and go home. Her shift was almost over, so she walked back to the private showing room to push in the chairs and clean up. His scent lingered in the air; for a moment, her chest ached with the familiar tightening of missing him.

The clock struck five. Liz punched her timecard, removed her designer high heels, placed them in their cotton dust bag, and slipped into her inexpensive boots. The snow was still coming down as she put on her threadbare coat, her wool hat, and gloves—all bought at the thrift store down the street from where she lived. Liz took the Metro card from her purse and put it in her coat pocket.

It was dark outside. Fifth Avenue decorated for Christmas had a special magic in the air, but Liz didn't even notice as she walked to the subway, hoping she could catch the five thirty train to Brooklyn and home. Her brain raced as she walked to the subway.

RICARDO ANTONIO DIMARCO sat in the back of his limousine next to Sofia Costello. He had no idea what the woman chatted on about—not since he had seen the salesclerk at the jewelry store. *My God, it was Liz! How could it be?* When he first saw her, he'd been surprised, but then he remembered his anger at Liz, and he wouldn't even acknowledge her. What would he have said to Sofia? Not that he owed anyone at any time an explanation for his behavior. He was, after all, a man who ran a multi-billion-dollar company. People did his bidding without question.

Sofia turned to him. "I enjoyed today. Will you be staying for dinner? Gianni should be home by now."

"No, as it happens, I have some last-minute business to take care of. I'm going to drop you home and then be on my way."

Sofia didn't have much more to say. Ricardo saw her to the door, greeted his brother Gianni, Sofia's fiancé, and then left.

The snow was coming down heavier now, as Ricardo's driver drove them toward his apartment on the upper east side of Manhattan. Ricardo dug into his coat pocket and pulled out his smartphone, punched a number, and called the head of his security. Keeping the anger that simmered in his belly from his voice, he said, "I would like some information on an Elizabeth Ferguson. I want a complete background check on her, *especially* what she has been doing for the past four years. I want a preliminary report within the hour, Joe." He ended the call and tried to relax. By the time they reached his apartment, his security chief had gotten him an address in Brooklyn. He told Ricardo that it wasn't in the best area, and it seemed that she lived alone. He would have more details for Ricardo in the morning.

He walked into his penthouse apartment to find dinner ready for him, made by his housekeeper. He bypassed the dining room and poured himself a whiskey, taking it to the master bedroom, removing his tie as he went. He wasn't hungry for food… he was hungry for revenge. Revenge on a beautiful petite redhead with curves that he still dreamt about.

"Grr," the growl escaped his lips. He didn't want to think of her, or her mouth kissing him, making him crazy as no one else had, ever. Holding the delicate crystal tumbler in his long fingers, he tipped the glass to his lips and downed the amber-colored liquid.

Entering the master bath, he reached into the glass-enclosed shower and turned the knob. Steam instantly filled the stall. He showered, then dressed in jeans and a heavy wool shirt. In his study with a fire blazing, he turned on his laptop. He googled Liz's address so he could know exactly where she lived. He sat at his computer, not seeing what he read any longer.

He saw her glorious red hair fanned out around that lethal body, while she sprawled across his bed, naked and waiting for him, with desire on that lovely face. The passion in those green cat eyes while she admired his naked body, made his desire rise.

God, he had loved her. He had never been in love before Liz and not since she had left him. He had wanted to marry that *strega tosico*, toxic witch. Give her his name, protect her, grow old with her. All the things his parents had. Now what? Seeing Liz again, he still wanted to bury himself in her, but all he would offer her now was to be his mistress, at his beck and call. He would make her pay for all the lies and deceit. Then when he was satisfied, he would be the one to walk out.

CHAPTER 2

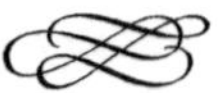

*L*iz found a seat as the train lurched forward, causing her to almost land on the man next to her. Her mind was on Ricardo, not seeing the other passengers around her.

Had the four years changed her that much? *He didn't even remember me. At one moment this afternoon, I thought he had. Maybe he didn't want his fiancée to know that we knew each other? That at one time, I had sat where Sofia had today.* Liz had dreamt of one day becoming his wife—they'd talked of marriage.

She was no longer the naive twenty-three-year-old he'd met five years ago after her parents had died. Her mother and father were only children, as was she, and their loss left her all alone in the world.

Feeling sorry for herself, Liz had decided to take a cruise to Bermuda. To think about her future and what she would do. That first night at dinner, she'd sat at a table with five fellow passengers, all single and traveling alone. They planned on meeting later, so after dinner, Liz went to the uppermost deck, wanting to walk under the stars. She didn't realize how windy it was out in the open until she stumbled and almost fell. Strong arms caught her. She steadied herself and peered into the black-as-night eyes of a tall, dark, and handsome man. His cheekbones looked to be chiseled by Michelangelo, his nose straight.

"Easy," he'd said. "Tonight is very windy, and you have to walk carefully on the deck." He had an accent; his voice sounded like gravel and gave her goosebumps.

"Oh, thank you. This is my first time on a ship. I wanted to come out and see the stars." She knew she was babbling. He smiled at her, still holding her in his arms. She looked up at him, trying to move out of his embrace. Then she stepped away.

"I know a place where you can look at the stars and not worry about being blown off the deck. Come, it's right here." She walked with him a few steps to an alcove that protected them from the wind. The night was clear and the stars an infinite blanket of twinkling points of light.

"Is it always this windy?" she'd asked.

"No, Bella. Tomorrow will be better, the perfect day for lying in the sun."

He had told her his name was Ricardo, and she had introduced herself. After she told him that she was traveling alone, he'd invited her to dinner the following evening. How she'd looked forward to meeting Ricardo for dinner.

That had been five years ago.

She got off at her stop. The commute home had taken much longer than expected. Liz walked through the snow toward her apartment building, where she saw a limousine covered with fresh snow parked out front. She stopped walking for a moment. Limousines in this area of Brooklyn were only for funerals, or a billionaire. Ignoring the alarm bells in her head shouting Rico, and ignoring the limo, she proceeded on her way. By the time she reached her building, the back passenger door opened, and Ricardo stepped out.

"Hello Liz."

She stopped. "How did you find me?"

"What? No hello? How are you? No, how have you been since I walked out on you? Nothing?" His anger vibrated in his voice, crystallizing his accent.

"I walked out on you?" she huffed. "Wasn't it the other way around? You were finished with me and moving on to new conquests. Now you're engaged."

His black brows lifted. Surprise showed on his face.

Liz clutched her threadbare coat closer, trying not to shiver.

"Come, let us go into your apartment. You're freezing."

She stiffened at his command. "No." She shook her head. "I can't. We have nothing to say to each other. You need to go." She glanced up at the building.

"Then get in the car. We're going to have a talk. Now!"

Telling her what to do. There it was, finally, the arrogance. She knew it wouldn't take long to surface. She was torn. What to do? She didn't want to get in the car, but she didn't want him in her home. She certainly didn't want him to meet Tony. Not now. Not ever.

Ignoring the wave of apprehension that swept through her, Liz reluctantly slid into the back of the limousine. He climbed in next to her, told his chauffeur to drive around the block, then he raised the privacy partition. The heater was on, making the interior warm and welcoming, but Liz sat ramrod straight, looking directly ahead, then she slowly glanced over at him. "Well, here I am, what do you want to talk about?"

He hadn't changed much in the four years since she'd seen him last. Maybe a few more lines around those expressive eyes. His jet-black hair was cut close to his head, shorter than he used to wear it. It was hard for her to keep the anger from her voice, vexed at just how much he had hurt her. And yes, how much she still missed him. Not a day went by that she didn't think about him. Think about what he'd so carelessly thrown away. Memories assailed her... how she'd run her fingers through the thickness of his hair and pulled his head closer to her body. She stopped those thoughts instantly.

With a contemptuous tone, he said, "I wanted to see how you were. I was under the impression you'd moved to France with your millionaire boyfriend Andre. What happened? Did he not give you enough money? Did you dump him too?"

Liz glanced out the car window. *What's he talking about?* The snow began sticking to the ground in earnest. At the rate it fell, there would be at least a foot of snow by morning. The first snow of the winter, and it was only early December. Liz turned back to look at him, shrugging one shoulder. "I never moved to France."

He grunted then his sculpted lips thinned, and his gaze held hers.

She couldn't turn away. "It's late. I have to go."

"You must be hungry. Come, let us have dinner."

"No. Actually, I'm not hungry. I have to get home now. Shouldn't you be getting back to your fiancée? When is the wedding?"

They circled the block two more times, and the limousine was about to go around again.

"Please let me out," she insisted. "There isn't anything for us to talk about." Why had she mentioned his fiancée? Would he think she cared?

She didn't—not anymore.

He said, sounding so calm, "Oh yes, Liz, there is much to talk about. Just for your information, I do not have a wedding date set."

She kept her tone even and flat, as if seeing him and being this close to him wasn't killing her. "I have to go now. Please don't look for me again." She waited for him to have the driver stop the car, so she could get out.

Instead, he said, "Tomorrow, we will have lunch... and talk further."

She met his brooding black eyes. "I'm working tomorrow. I will not have lunch with you." Trying to keep the quiver from her voice, she said, "Let me out."

"You do know, Liz, that with just one phone call, I can have you dismissed from your employment?"

He never raised his tone, he just stated a fact she knew to be true. He was that powerful. There it was, the brute threatening her, *just* as his Aunt Angela had.

"I—"

No, she wasn't going to think about that. She wouldn't let him see her fear. She had to get away from him, she had to get to Tony.

"Ricardo—"

"You used to call me Rico, remember?" His husky whisper sent heat up her spine, taking the chill of fear away.

She remembered a lot more than that... A memory flashed before her, of when he met her for dinner, that night so long ago, on his cruise ship. She'd worn a black form-fitting cocktail dress that still hung in her closet as she was unable to part with it. He'd brought her to his suite where a dinner of lobster and steak had waited for them. She'd been surprised that he'd had such an elaborate suite. He'd told her that he was one of the owners of the cruise line, and he wasn't on vacation, but on an inspection. He'd taken her hand, and they'd walked out onto the balcony. The inky darkness of the night sky had been so like his eyes.

RICARDO SAT in the limousine next to Liz, deep in his own thoughts. He drank in her beauty, the pert little nose, those sensuous full lips, almost too big for her face, but just right. Especially when she had used them to kiss down his body.

Too bad she had turned out to be a gold-digging liar. He found it difficult to believe she could change so much. How had she turned into such a fraud? He'd loved her. They'd dated for several months after returning from the cruise. One night back at her apartment, he'd breathed near her ear, "Tonight, *Cara mia*, you will be mine." He'd kissed her then, a long hard kiss, picking her up and carrying her to the bed. He'd known she was innocent, but she was so *sensual*, he'd been surprised to find her a virgin. Soon after that, she'd moved into his penthouse. He'd loved her and no other. She thought he was engaged to Sofia, and he was happy to let her think that.

Her voice broke into his thoughts, "Ricardo, it's late. I have to get home. Please have your driver stop the car and let me go."

"Not until you agree to have lunch with me tomorrow."

"Fine, I will have lunch with you. Now *stop* the car."

Ricardo tapped on the privacy window, and his driver pulled the limo over to the curb. Before Ricardo could get out, she climbed past him and ran up the walkway into her building.

He watched her disappear from his sight, ready to tell his driver to take him home when he noticed that she had left her purse on the floor of the limousine.

CHAPTER 3

*L*iz ran up the five flights of stairs trying to calm herself before she walked into the tiny apartment.

She didn't want her son Tony to see her upset. She unlocked the door and pushed it open. The aroma of home-made bread and stew wafted through the house.

"Mama, you're home." Tony scooted off the sofa, his arms outstretched as he scampered toward her in his heavy flannel Thomas the Train pajamas.

"How's my boy?" She bent down to pick him up, breathing in his fresh baby powder scent.

He hugged her. "I missed you, Mama. *Nonna* said if I'm good, we can play in the snow tomorrow."

"That will be so much fun. Did you eat your dinner?"

He nodded. His mop of black curls bounced up and down, and a big smile formed on his bow lips. "Yes, Mama, and now I'm ready for bed. Will you read me a story?"

Anna Carducci came into the living room, wearing her nightgown and a robe. Her silver-streaked brown hair was up in a bun, her warm, brown eyes offering comfort to Liz, much like Liz's mother had done when she'd been alive.

"Oh Tony, I'll read you a story, so that your mama can rest and have her dinner."

His face scrunched up, and he shook his head. "No, I want Mama to read." Then he rubbed his eyes, and Liz smiled at him.

Anna said, "We were at the park, and now he's fighting to stay awake."

"I'll carry you to your room, and then *Nonna* can read to you. I will kiss you good night after your story. Will that be all right?"

He smiled and hugged Liz's neck, and she walked into his bedroom.

Anna followed Liz down the dark, narrow hall. "Are you okay? Is everything all right? It's late. Were the trains not running on schedule because of the snow?"

"I'm okay, Anna… just tired."

"There's stew in the kitchen and homemade bread."

"I smelled it when I came in." Liz smiled at Tony and kissed him on the cheek. "I'll be back after I eat."

Anna whispered, "I think we may both be asleep by then." She went over to his nightstand and picked up a book. "Tony, let's read your favorite story."

Liz ruffled her son's head of black curls, closed the bedroom door, and as she walked down the hall to the kitchen, a memory of the day she had met Anna came to her. Liz had been six months pregnant with Tony, with a low-income job and no health insurance. She'd rented a room in a house after the breakup. When she could no longer afford to pay the rent, her landlord had asked Liz to vacate the room. Liz understood and packed her meager belongings. With nowhere to go, she'd sat on a park bench in Brooklyn, near where she'd lived. Tears streamed down her cheeks, Anna had sat next to her and handed Liz a tissue.

"Thank you," Liz sniffed.

"I've seen you around the neighborhood. Is everything all right?"

Before she realized it, Liz had told Anna the whole story. How the father of her baby didn't want her or the baby and how she had no place to go. The older woman offered Liz a room in her apartment. After Tony was born, Anna took care of him so that Liz could return to work.

They lived in a one-and-a-half-bedroom apartment on the fifth floor of a building without an elevator. Tony's bedroom was big enough for his bed and a dresser. Liz slept on the pullout couch in the living room. Many nights, Tony ended up sleeping with her. She knew how much he missed her, but she had to work. Anna never asked her for money, and Liz helped pay a portion of the rent as well as the groceries.

Liz walked to the kitchen to plate her dinner. There was a knock at the door, so she put the dish on the kitchen counter and went to the entry. She rose on tiptoe and peered through the peephole. Ricardo was at her apartment door.

Oh no, it's him. What does he want? Liz had to get rid of Ricardo right away.

She opened the door but left the security chain on. Ricardo stood there, so handsome. Her chest ached, reminding her of how he'd broken her heart.

He held up her handbag. "I think you will need this."

She pushed in the door to unlatch the chain and opened it just enough to put out her hand for her purse. One of his eyebrows lifted.

"Will you let me in?" he asked in his deep, sexy voice.

"It's late. I can't. I need to get up extra early tomorrow to get into the city on time, because of the snow… and all. I'm sure it will be a long commute." *What if Tony comes out?*

"The snow has stopped but if you are worried, I will send a car for you. Let me in, Liz."

She hesitated. *Just for a minute. I can't be rude.* Then Liz stepped out of the way. Ricardo entered her apartment. She glanced down the hall.

He sat on the thread-bare sofa that was covered in an afghan Anna had crocheted. His custom-made coat was unbuttoned to reveal his wool shirt and denim jeans. Italian leather loafers were on his feet. "I remember when you were eager to invite me into your home and into your bed."

Liz smirked. If only he knew how close he was to her bed. "That was in another lifetime, Rico."

She swallowed past the lump in her throat—she'd just called him Rico, not Ricardo. Liz couldn't get comfortable with him again. He was engaged to someone else.

He removed his coat and folded it over the back of the couch. He looked relaxed sitting there in his jeans and shirt.

"Did I interrupt dinner? It smells good."

Her eyes shifted to the hall and back to him. She couldn't resist this chance to be near him… and the kitchen was the farthest from the bedroom. "Yes, would you like some? It isn't much. Just beef stew and bread."

"Yes, thank you. I haven't had dinner yet."

Liz led the way into the kitchen, using her chin to point to the table covered with a clean but faded green tablecloth. "Take a seat." She grabbed a bowl from the kitchen cabinet. Looking at it, she frowned and put it to the side. She took out another and examined it before she ladled the stew inside. Next were two glasses that she filled with water and placed one by each bowl. She then put bread on a cutting board.

He tasted the stew and looked up at her. "This is quite good, Liz. Is the bread homemade?"

Liz sat at the table. *It was a mistake to invite him in.* He was so handsome with his black as night hair and his eyes which never revealed anything.

"Yes, it is, but I didn't make it. I work all day and then–I–I come home tired." Oh dear, she'd almost said, 'and then I come home and take care of my son.' Her thoughts were wild. *What does he want from me?* There was no nice small talk between them, not the way there had been when she had loved him. Before he had betrayed her and broken her heart.

"What happened to you? Why are you living in this… this broken-down apartment?" He motioned with both arms outstretched. "In this neighborhood, which isn't safe."

The frustration in his voice couldn't be missed. Liz put her spoon down and pushed her plate away. She went to the stove and filled the espresso pot with water and coffee. Anna, being Italian, loved her espresso and had taught Liz how to make it. She knew Rico would be surprised that she could make the rich brew. Once the flame was on the coffee maker, she turned back to him. "You know I used my inheritance to pay my student loans."

"Liz, what happened with the Frenchman—"

She thought for a moment. "Who?"

"Andre Bourbon, the Frenchman who was on *my* ship."

"Nothing happened between us. I didn't even know him. He was a guest on your ship. I had *nothing* to do with him—"

"You slept with him!" He shoved his fingers in his hair.

"How could I sleep with someone I didn't even know?" Liz kept her voice low and tried not to show how upset he'd made her by that accusation.

When the coffee was ready, she poured it into a cup then added sugar, just the way she remembered he liked it.

He took the espresso cup from her hands and drank the dark brew down in one gulp. "So beautiful," he whispered, "and so deceitful." He stared into her eyes. "I saw you in bed with him." His lip curled. "You are a liar and a slut."

She raised her hand—he caught her wrist only inches away from slapping him. He twisted her arm behind her back, and she tried to break free. He pulled her tight against his hard body, bending his head.

She turned her face away. "Ricardo!"

"Damn you and your faithless body." His hand roamed over her buttock, dragging her into him, his other hand reached up to hold her chin in place for his kiss. He groaned and bent his head. He ran his tongue along the seam of her compressed lips and nibbled at the corner of her mouth. He kissed down her neck. She sighed, and he let go of her wrist at the same time his lips moved back to hers. Now she opened them for him. He took full advantage and caressed her tongue with his. His fingers reached into her hair, and she stood on her toes to fit more fully against him. He lifted her into his body, her feet no longer touching the floor.

Her arms wrapped around his neck, and her fingers ran through his hair. He smelled so good. What his mouth did to her—she clung to his body. She missed him so much. She needed this, she needed him. Her feet touched the floor, and Liz heard the rasp as Ricardo slipped the zipper down the back of her dress. She pushed at his chest, pulling away from him.

"No," she said, in a shaky voice, mortified by her reaction to his demanding kiss. How could she fall so quickly into his arms? Her brain screamed—*he's engaged to someone else.* She hated herself almost as much as she hated him.

Ricardo looked confused. His eyes became two black slits, his face stone. Liz saw true fury.

"Still up to your old tricks? Is that what happened with the Frenchman? He saw you for what you are, a slu–"

"Don't you call me that again. Look at you, engaged to another woman and trying to get me into bed. Well, I am no longer a starry-eyed, naive virgin who thought the sun rose and set around you." She flashed him a look of disdain.

He cut in. "Is that what you were? I think you saw a

chance to marry into money, so you pretended to care for me. You almost made it Liz; another month and we would have been married."

She shook her head and looked at him. *He would never understand.* "It's late. You'd better run along to your fiancée. I have to get to sleep. I need to be up early for work."

"Oh yes, you work *now*. Well then, I will bid you good night, Liz." Ricardo turned on his heel and walked from the kitchen into the living room. He picked his coat up from the sofa and strode out the door.

Liz let out her breath, not realizing she'd held it. Her body shook as she walked to the door and turned the dead bolt then slid the security chain back into place. She tiptoed down the hall.

Anna's bedroom door was still closed, and Liz didn't see any glow from her lamp. She breathed a sigh of relief as she checked on Tony. The corners of her mouth lifted. He was asleep in his red race car bed. The headlights acted as a nightlight, and they were on, casting a soft glow around the small room. She'd bought him that bed for his third birthday just six months ago. He hugged his teddy bear in his sleep. She bent and kissed his cheek, then she tiptoed out of his room, closing the door behind her. She opened the sleeper couch in the living room and then went to change.

Her meager supply of clothes hung in the standing wardrobe. Opening the door, she removed her nightgown. Liz hung up her work outfit. The designer dress and shoes had cost her a month's salary. She remembered how Anna had persuaded her to buy the right clothes to land the job in the expensive jewelry store on Fifth Avenue. She'd been right.

Liz ran her open hand over her clothes, ignoring the black cocktail dress hidden in the back. The rest of her outfits were all secondhand and some not nearly warm enough for the winter. The dress and shoes were the only luxuries she could afford for herself. When Ricardo left her pregnant and alone, she couldn't find a job with health insurance. She'd used the remainder of her inheritance and sold some of her nicer clothes. She'd owed the hospital and the doctor who'd delivered Tony. Then to make matters worse, the economy had taken a dive.

All her money went to dress and feed Tony. She'd skipped meals so he could eat better quality food. She bought him the best of everything. No second-hand clothes from the thrift shop for her little boy. She had been working at this job for a few months. The pay was much better than her previous job. Now she had health insurance for herself and Tony, so she hoped to be out of debt soon.

Even if his father didn't want him, she loved him and would always provide the best for *her* son. He was her world. She was grateful that Rico hadn't seen him. Should Ricardo ever meet Tony, he would know instantly that the little boy was his son. Tony's hair and eyes were just as black as his father's. Liz huddled under the blanket on her bed and tried not to think of Rico.

She still felt his lips on hers; it was impossible not to think of him. She sighed. *He'd grown more handsome if that were possible.* Her heart contracted, remembering all they had shared. Why had he asked her about Andre? She didn't understand.

Ricardo knew she'd met the man at the same time he had. They were on one of Ricardo's ships, relaxing at the pool. Andre had been there, and he started a conversation with Rico. They discussed wine from the different regions of Italy. That evening, the three of them had dinner together. After the cruise, Andre had gone home to Paris, and she never saw him again.

She wished things had been different between Rico and

her. The way he said her name, with his accent, in his sexy gravelly voice. *Leeza.* He'd whispered her name in the night while making love to her. He'd introduced her to passion, and tonight when she'd seen him again, she realized how much she'd missed him. She hugged her pillow close, her throat tight with tears, and cried for all the misunderstandings.

"Mama, Mama," Tony called from his room.

Liz got out of bed and went to him. "Darling, what's wrong?"

"Water, please. I want a drink," he said.

She bent down and lifted Tony from his toddler bed, carrying him to the kitchen, where she set him down at the table and poured him a glass of water. He drank it and then lifted his arms for his mother to pick him up.

"Can I sleep with you, Mama?"

She cuddled him close. "You want to sleep with me? Sure, handsome." Liz snuggled her son next to her on the sleeper sofa and was finally able to fall asleep.

Just before her alarm clock rang, Liz woke up. The radiator whistled as the heat rose in the apartment. She glanced to the living room window to see the panes foggy and the bottom corners covered with frost. Liz carried Tony back to his bed, kissed his warm cheek, and dressed for work. She rushed out of the apartment, not wanting to be late.

With yesterday's snowfall and this morning's bitter cold, she wished the trains were on time. She really needed this job. When Liz arrived at work, the manager Jonathan Doyle met her at the door.

"Good morning, Miss Ferguson. Would you come into my office?" He never smiled but today, he looked especially grim.

"Certainly, sir." Liz followed him into his office with dread.

"Don't bother closing the door," he said as he turned to her.

Mr. Doyle didn't allow her to sit. "Miss Ferguson, I'm going to have to let you go. I have already drawn your final paycheck." He held out an envelope for her to take.

Liz looked down at the envelope, then back up to her boss. "I… I don't understand. Is there a problem with my work?" Panic rose from the pit of her stomach, and a knot of fear choked her.

"You are being dismissed. Please empty your locker and go before the store opens. Jim from security will escort you."

Liz turned, not realizing anyone else was in the office. Jim stood at the door. She took a breath and despite the tears that already stung the back of her eyes, swore she wouldn't cry. Mr. Doyle jerked the envelope toward her. Her hand shook as she grabbed it and walked out of his office.

With a lump in her throat, Liz held back her tears. Her voice cracked as she said to Jim, "I don't have anything in my locker."

He nodded and escorted her to the front door. Her shoulders hunched over. Tears filled her eyes, about to spill onto her cheeks as she stepped out into the brisk early morning air. Wrapping her coat tighter around her, she turned her collar up against the bitter cold.

Traffic crawled by. Smoke from the car exhausts rose into the air and along the concrete sidewalk, some wet spots where salt had been spread, melted the ice. Parked in front of the store was a black stretch limousine, nothing unusual for Fifth Avenue. As she walked out onto the icy sidewalk, the back door opened and out stepped Ricardo. She stopped short. "You!" she shouted. "You did this to me." Her tears were replaced by a burning anger.

He held the door open, his voice gruff. "Get in."

"What? Why should I? I can't believe that you did this. *You* did this to me." She grabbed the lapels of his custom-made cashmere coat, her fists pulling the fabric to shake him. "Don't you know I have nothing? I don't know how I will survive."

"Get in the car. I have a proposition for you." He covered her hands as she gripped his lapels. He didn't try to remove them. "Come, it's cold out. That coat you have on cannot possibly keep you warm."

A tear slid down her cheek.

His lips compressed, and he grunted before his thumb wiped at her cheek. Liz moved away. "No."

"I see you shivering. Do not be obstinate." Ricardo took her hands off his coat. "Come, you're freezing. Get in the car, you are too stubborn for your own good." He helped her into the backseat and slid in next to her. Liz scooted away from him.

Once Ricardo shut the back door, his driver pulled into the morning rush hour traffic.

Liz's body was tense—she'd just been fired, and Christmas was only a few weeks away. The plush interior invited her to sink into the seat, and the heater kept the chill out. She wiped the tears off her cheeks with the back of her hand. Liz hated crying in front of Ricardo. He had something to do with her getting fired. She *knew* that. But why? *Because he believes I cheated on him with Andre. I couldn't do that, I'd loved him. Now, well, now I hate him.*

He shifted in the seat. Liz glanced at Ricardo. "I know you had me fired. Why? How could you? You've taken everything away from me."

She silently vowed not to cry anymore and turned away from his icy stare. Her brows came together as she glanced out the dark-tinted window. "Where are you taking me?" She couldn't hide the panic in her voice as she noticed they were heading toward the Holland Tunnel out of the city to New Jersey.

Black, fathomless eyes stared at her as Ricardo said, "We're going for a ride, so that we can talk. You remember I have a house in Jersey? Relax. We will be there soon."

She needed to get away from him. She had to get home to Tony. Somehow, she would have to get her son and leave the city. Her mind raced. On the outside, she tried for calm as she sat on the leather seat. The limo crawled in the morning traffic.

Where can I go? I have so little money. She hated Ricardo for what he had done to her. Wasn't it bad enough she would never know his touch again, that he was marrying someone else—that he'd have children with another woman? He would love those children and never know her son. She had to get out of the limousine. She had to get out. *Now!* Could she unlock the door and slide out while they were stopped at the red light?

Liz ignored the fear that consumed her—she had to escape. She scooched over to the door. She didn't care anymore; she needed to run from Ricardo. She grabbed the handle, lifted it, and pushed against the door.

"Merda," he cursed. "What are you doing?"

She felt the tug on her coat and heard the rip of the fabric as he tried to pull her back into the car, but he was too late— Liz was out. She ran in front of the limo and down the street onto the icy sidewalk. She slipped, tried to catch her balance but couldn't, and fell, almost back into the gutter, nearly getting hit by a car.

The car's horn blared, drowning out her scream.

Suddenly, Ricardo was at her side. He bent down and scooped her up into his strong arms. He shouted in anger, "What the hell are you trying to do? Kill yourself?"

He stalked back to the limo. His driver had the door open,

and Ricardo put Liz on the seat, getting in next to her. "You are foolish to think you can escape me."

"Please. I can't go to New Jersey. I have to get home. Please, Rico." She was hysterical, no longer caring about the tears that streamed down her cheeks, or that he saw her weakness.

Rico pressed the intercom button, and he told his driver, "Change of plans. Take us to Brooklyn."

CHAPTER 4

$\mathcal{A}$s the stretch limo drove toward Brooklyn, Liz allowed Rico to take her onto his lap, so he could examine her skinned knees.

"Take off your pantyhose." Rico reached for the first aid kit his driver had gotten from the trunk. "Take them off now," his voice softened, "or is it that you want me to do it?"

At that threat, Liz scrambled off his lap, and with as much dignity as possible, shimmied the ripped hose down past her knees. He dragged her legs across his lap and dabbed antiseptic on her scraped knees. She winced at the sting.

"What possessed you to jump out of the car like that? Did you think I was going to hurt you? I just want to talk with you." He stopped what he was doing and glanced at her.

She wouldn't look at him. It was bad enough she had to subject herself to his gentle care. "I have a way for you to make up to me for all of your deceit," he said as he placed a clean bandage on her knee.

Liz shifted her eyes to glance at him but decided not to say anything.

~

Ricardo studied Liz, her eyes downcast and her glorious mane of red hair coming loose from the bun. What was going on with her? She wore an expensive dress, though it appeared similar to the one she had on yesterday. Her coat wouldn't keep *anyone* warm, and now there was a rip where he'd tried to grab her before she ran out of the car. Her boots were old and scuffed, the leather worn thin. Now, they were also wet from the snow. He finished bandaging her knees, and she moved her legs off his lap.

Liz leaned back on the seat. "You have to let me go," she said, her voice devoid of expression.

"Not before you tell me what you have been doing. Where are you spending all your money? You are single, you make a nice salary at the jewelry store—"

"*Made* a nice salary. Remember *you* had me fired," she sniffed.

He almost growled at her, his voice rough, "Be grateful that is all I have done."

She lifted her chin then waved her hand in the air. "Oh, please, I don't want to argue with you anymore."

"That is the first sensible thing you have said today." He helped her remove her coat and drew her onto his lap. This time she didn't struggle.

"Ricardo, let me go." She rested her palm against his chest and muttered, "You're engaged."

His hand engulfed her daintier one as he said, "Ah, *si*. I guess… I should tell you about Sofia. You remember my younger brother Gianni? Do you not?"

"Of course, I remember him. He was always nice to me."

"Well, you see… Sofia is his fiancée."

Her head snapped up, and she looked at him. "Oh."

Her beautiful mouth so close to his, he couldn't help

himself. He had to have another sample, just to prove to himself that her lips weren't as overpowering as he thought. Who was he kidding? He felt her hesitation, but he was insistent, and she opened her lips to his demanding kiss.

Her taste reminded him of Sicily, hot delicious honey. Liz relaxed against him. With the privacy partition up and the dark, tinted windows, she kissed him back. His tongue traced the soft fullness of her lips. She parted her lips, and his tongue darted in to explore the recesses of her mouth. She entwined her tongue with his, and time evaporated. She was in his arms again, her sensuous mouth making demands of her own. These were the kisses he remembered and no other compared.

Ricardo held her on his lap as they made their way back to Brooklyn.

He breathed against her lips. "I wanted to take you away, someplace where we can be alone." He held her, kissing her neck. "My penthouse, as well as Gianni's apartment, are full of guests from Sicily. They are Christmas shopping before we all fly back to Palermo for the holidays. I wanted to talk privately with you." He nuzzled her throat and ran his fingers through her silky mass of red hair. Gliding the zipper down her back, he tugged her dress to her waist. In the warmth of the backseat, he dragged her against his chest. His tongue licked her satin skin as he moved to her sensuous lips. He studied her closely. She was beautiful, though thinner than he remembered. He frowned. *Too thin.*

Liz glanced down and turned away from him. She lifted her dress to cover herself, slipping one arm into a sleeve and then the other. Liz reached around and began to zip up the dress. He brushed her fingers away and finished zipping the dress. She slipped off his lap and turned her head toward the window.

Ricardo tipped his head to one side. Surprised by her

thinness and the rags she wore under the expensive dress. He expected a lace and satin bra, but to see cotton, that wasn't bad; it was the fact it was dingy and gray from wear that surprised him. "Liz, what the hell has become of you?"

Her head came up, her eyes blazed. "You happened to me, that's what happened," she snapped, "Four years ago, *you* threw me out of your apartment and your life. Now you get me fired, and I will probably lose this apartment, all because of you."

The limousine pulled up in front of her building. "Ricardo, let me out," she said coolly, "so I can go back to my life."

Ricardo reached for the door handle but hesitated. "I want to talk to you. Come with me to—"

She shook her head. "No, never!"

His anger built—nobody ever said no to him. That word, no, he didn't acknowledge unless he used it. He glanced down at his solid-gold, ultra-thin wristwatch, and his lips formed a straight line.

"This is not over, Liz. We *will* talk, but not now." He helped her out of the car and began to walk her to the building door.

"No, don't. You go." She lifted her hand and made a dismissive gesture as she walked away from Ricardo. He had no choice but to let her go.

He didn't care what would become of me four years ago when he threw me out of his home. Why does he care now? Once their relationship had become serious, Ricardo had persuaded her to give up her home, even her job, and move in with him. She loved him, and they spoke of a future together… then she found herself on the street. The way he'd done it still stung. He'd sent his Aunt Angela to tell her she had to get out. That

Ricardo wanted her out of his penthouse that very night. She had left everything he bought her—clothes and jewelry, she'd left it all behind. That was the *worst* day of her life.

Now, she forced herself not to glance back at Rico. Her shoulders hunched over.

The familiar pain of betrayal burned as she climbed the stairs and walked into her apartment.

"Liz, what has happened? You ripped your coat." Anna looked surprised to see her home so early. She said her name just like Rico did… they had the same accent. Before Liz could answer, Tony turned onto his tummy and slid off the couch. He ran into her arms.

"Mama, look… snow. I want to go play."

She ruffled his head of black curls. "After lunch, okay?"

"Okay." Tony climbed onto the couch to watch his favorite DVD on the small TV.

Anna, with a fresh pot of American coffee in her hand, poured Liz a cup. Liz sat on the wooden chair at the kitchen table and stared into the mug.

Concern showed on Anna's face. "What's wrong? Last night, I hear a man's voice in the house. In all the years, I know you, Liz, you never date or bring a man home."

Liz looked up at Anna. "I got fired today. I have no idea how I'm going to take care of Tony, or help you pay the rent."

Anna's eyes rounded. "I know you a hard worker." She patted Liz's hand. "You do not think about it today. Tomorrow, you will begin looking for another job. We will make everything work out." The older woman got up from her chair and put her arms around Liz. "You eat now, then you take Tony out to play in the snow. I gonna fix your coat."

Liz made herself a peanut butter and jelly sandwich. For Tony, she broiled a chicken leg and steamed his favorite vegetables, peas and carrots.

After lunch, she put on her heaviest pair of pants and

both the sweatshirts she owned. She'd placed her boots near the radiator to dry. She pulled them on over heavy wool socks. Tony was already dressed, so she got his snowsuit, waterproof boots, and thick wool hat with the matching scarf and mittens. There was enough snow on the ground for his sled, so she took that out of the closet.

When he saw the sled, he jumped up and down with excitement. "Yay, are you going to pull me, Mama?"

"Yes, handsome."

Anna was going to the grocery store to stock up on milk and other staples, as the forecast now said a blizzard was imminent. Liz walked the several blocks to the park, pulling Tony on his sled, which had been last year's Christmas present from Santa. She'd gone to the largest toy store in New York City to purchase it for him. What would she do this year? Christmas was only three weeks away, and now she had no job. She hated Ricardo for having her fired and then just driving off to his meeting. What did he care with all his billions of dollars? He had no idea how she'd suffered. Went without so her son—his son—could have the best.

She never wanted Tony to know that his father was a brute. Tony had started to ask questions, like where his dad lived. He saw other children at the park with a mama and a daddy. Liz thought she'd have more time before she had to explain that he only had her and no daddy.

Her heart wrenched. Her poor little boy would never know the love of a father. Maybe she should start dating and find a stepdad for Tony. Each time she thought of that, Rico's handsome face came to mind, haunting her. She couldn't even think of another man touching her. Making love to her.

A fine snow fell and stuck to the ground—cold permeated through her, and Liz realized they'd been at the park for three hours. No wonder she couldn't feel her toes. As she pulled the sled and Tony toward home, a black limousine pulled up to her apartment building.

"Ugh," she groaned. Panic gripped her insides, she almost turned around. The limo door opened, and Ricardo emerged from the backseat. He stared at her.

"Car, Mama, big car."

"Yes, darling, a big car." *And a big man with a scowl on his face.* A scowl she could see even from this distance.

He walked up to them, snow swirling over his fancy Italian shoes.

"Hello Liz."

Liz picked up Tony and his sled. Ignoring Ricardo, she climbed the steps and went into the building. Ricardo followed and took the sled from her ice-cold hands.

Tony looked at Ricardo. "Hello. Are you my daddy?"

Liz stiffened. That was his new question to every man he met. The *Stranger Danger* talk she'd had with him hadn't stuck. She carried Tony up the stairs, glancing to the side. Ricardo was a step behind, so he could look directly at Tony. Liz was sure that Ricardo couldn't see more than Tony's eyes, the way she'd bundled him up against the cold New York winter.

"Hello young man. What is your name?"

"Tony. We played at the park."

Liz reached her apartment and unlocked the door. She didn't look at Ricardo but left the door open. She set Tony on the sofa and unzipped his bright-red snowsuit. She crouched down and took off his boots and his mittens. Tony chatted on and on with Ricardo.

"Would you like some milk and a cookie?" Tony gave her a big smile and a nod, then reached to yank on his hat fastener. Liz had no choice and finally took the hat off her son's head, revealing black curls. She waited, but there was no reaction from Ricardo. She smiled to herself and hoped something good might come out of this day after all. Tony scooted off the sofa and ran into the kitchen. Liz followed and helped him climb onto a chair. Ricardo leaned one shoulder against the kitchen doorframe.

"Mama, can I have chocolate milk?"

Ricardo jerked away from the doorframe. "*What?*" His voice was hard, his stance ominous.

Liz ignored him and said calmly, "Yes, darling. Mama will make you chocolate milk."

She glanced through the fringe of her lashes at Ricardo. His face was a mask of rage, his nostrils flaring. The air crackled with his fury.

"How old is he, Liz? I see you didn't waste any time with Andre. Wasn't he blond?"

She stopped mid-pour and raised her eyes to him. "I told you I was never with him."

Liz placed the glass of milk on the table. "Careful, darling, use two hands." She put a cookie on a napkin in front of Tony.

"So that's why Andre is not with you now? You didn't waste any time finding another lover."

Liz shook her head at Ricardo and whispered, "Shh, please... my son." She stayed near Tony while he ate his cookie. When he'd finished his snack, Liz said, "Let's go into the bedroom for your nap."

"I don't want to."

Liz bent close and frowned. "*T o n y...*"

He hung his head, then slipped off the chair, and waved his chubby fingers at Ricardo, following his mother down the hall to his room. Liz unbuttoned his outfit and laid him in his red race car bed. She covered him with a blanket, then kissed his cheek, and he went right to sleep. Closing the bedroom door, she stood tall and mumbled, "Now, to face the bear in the living room."

Ricardo dwarfed the room. A lock of black hair fell over his forehead, and her hand itched to push it back into place.

His ebony eyebrows pulled together, frowning at her with black-as night eyes she could get lost in.

"What do you want from me?"

"Tell me about… your… little boy."

Liz shrugged her shoulder. "What's to tell?" She wouldn't look at his lips; she missed the feel of them on her body.

"Do not be that way with me, Liz. You know what I mean. Where is his father? Who do you leave him with when you work?"

Liz watched him from across the room. "He doesn't have a father. He has me. His father didn't want him." She moved to sit on the couch.

"How could a father not want his son? Did he let you go when he found out?"

"Yes, something like that. I have things to do. I would like you to go now." She stood and walked toward the door.

He grabbed her arm. "I am not going yet. We haven't finished our talk. If it wasn't Andre, then who? How many men have you been with?" His face became a mask of rage, and his eyes burned into her as if he wanted to read her mind.

She refused to flinch and yanked her arm away. "How many men? How many you ask? Well, none. None of your business. That's how many." Liz hissed the words at him.

His lip curled, and he cursed in Italian. He dragged her into his embrace, and his mouth captured hers. It wasn't a gentle kiss but hard and demanding.

Rico crushed her to him, his lips searching. Liz tried to push away but he held her tighter.

~

RICARDO WANTED HER TO SURRENDER. Liz drove him crazy—he wanted her on her knees, begging him to take her back, to give her sweet body only to him. He cupped her head to hold her still, kissing the corners of her mouth, but she wouldn't open to him. *Oh, but you will and more before I'm done with you.*

He ran his tongue along the seam of her lips. His hand went under the rough layers of sweatshirts and touched the satin skin of her waist. He reached higher and kissed a trail down her neck. He moved his hand from her head, brought it around her back, and unclasped her bra. Her ragged intake of breath didn't stop him. She didn't protest. He ran both thumbs along her taut nipples.

He kissed her lips again. This time there was no resistance, and her warm, honeyed mouth opened for him... he thrust his tongue into the sweetness. One hand left a breast and moved down her back into the waistband of her panties to cup the curve of her buttock. She moaned into his mouth and lifted herself up to get closer. He tasted her surrender; he was already hard. He had never stopped wanting her. He pressed against her soft body. He wanted her right now! No. No, he would take her at his leisure in one of his homes. Not in this dilapidated apartment, with the boy sleeping in the next room. Is this what she had become? Easy?

He pushed her away. "Fix yourself. I will not bed you here. Your *son* is in the next room."

Her hand trembled as it rose to her mouth. A mouth that was moist from his kisses. Liz looked mortified as she covered her lips. He knew Liz would have let him make love to her right there on the couch or even the floor, whatever he wanted. She turned from him, pulled her shirt down, and smoothed her hair, combing her fingers through the tangles.

The entry door opened. Liz groaned. "Oh, no." An older woman walked into the apartment with a bag of groceries in her arms. Liz rushed over to her and took the bag, bringing it to the kitchen. The older woman stared at him but before he could say anything. Liz hurried back to the living room. She looked between him and the woman and then said, "Ricardo, I would like you to meet Anna Carducci, my friend, and the woman who takes care of Tony."

He extended his hand to Anna.

Anna clasped his palm. "It is nice that you have come to meet your son."

CHAPTER 5

Ricardo stiffened. His son? His head snapped toward Liz. Her green eyes darted back and forth in fear, and he knew it was true. Growling, his teeth clenched, and he marched down the narrow hall, reaching the bedroom in two strides. The sound of Liz's hurried footsteps followed.

Tony slept in a red race car bed that didn't fit with the depressed state of the apartment. His bow lips were slightly parted, and his long eyelashes lay against rosy cheeks. His black-as-night hair was tousled with curls.

Ricardo looked at Liz in wonderment. He knew it was true. This little boy who slept so peacefully was his son. He had a son. A son! He walked back into the living room, Liz on his heels.

Ricardo was livid with rage but kept his voice low and even, "So, you weren't going to tell me?"

Liz stood with her arms crossed over her chest, her chin lifted in defiance.

"How much longer will he sleep?"

"Maybe a half hour," she mumbled.

"Pack your things." He pointed to her outfit. "And none of those rags." He took out his cell phone, dialed a number, and spoke in rapid Italian. Ricardo finished his call then texted a message. Shortly after that, his phone pinged. He glanced down at the screen.

Tony came out of the bedroom rubbing his eyes. When he saw Ricardo, he grinned. "You're here!"

Liz blew out her breath and rolled her eyes. "Come, let's go to the bathroom, so you can brush your teeth, and I can comb your hair."

"Can I have a cookie, Mama?"

"Yes, darling, after your hair." Tony scooted ahead of Liz into the bathroom. He brushed his teeth while Liz combed his hair. When he was done, he ran toward the kitchen. "No running," Liz said.

He walked into the kitchen, climbed onto one of the chairs, and waited for his cookie.

Ricardo hunkered down on his haunches next to Tony. He put one arm over the back of the chair and asked, "Do you remember my car?"

Tony held his cookie in both hands, his eyes round. "Big car."

"Yes, it is. Would you like to go for a ride in it?"

"Can Mama and *Nonna* come too?"

Despite his fury, Ricardo sounded smooth, almost cheerful, "Of course, they can."

Liz panicked, her hand to her throat. *What if he takes Tony, and I never see him again?* Fear gripped her. *Would Rico do that? Would he?*

"You finish while I go talk to your mama. Okay?"

Tony held the cookie in his chubby fingers and smiled at Rico as he nodded his head.

Rico stood and followed Liz into the living room. "You and Tony are coming with me *now*." He looked at Anna. "Signora Carducci, if you would like to join us, you are welcome too."

"Where are you taking us?" Liz asked, her voice anxious.

"My personal assistant is booking us into a suite at the Plaza Hotel."

Despite her reluctance to do as he wanted, Liz dressed Tony in his snowsuit. Why a hotel? She and Anna put on their coats and walked down the steps to the waiting limousine. Ricardo followed, carrying his son. The driver opened the back door.

They drove in silence, except for Tony, who had so many questions. Ricardo answered every one of his son's questions. He chuckled at him and ruffled Tony's hair from time to time. The limousine arrived at the entrance to the world-famous hotel. The driver came around and opened the back door. Ricardo's personal assistant Massimo met them and escorted the group through the main lobby. "There is a private entrance, but I thought your guests would like to see the Christmas tree and all the decorations." Massimo looked at Liz. "It is nice to see you again, Miss Ferguson."

"Thank you, but you *always* called me Liz." She smiled at him. The older man dipped his head of silver hair, then cleared his throat and glanced at Ricardo. Ricardo didn't say anything, just nodded that they should continue. His PA led the way past a bank of elevators, up marble steps with a thick red carpet runner down the center.

They proceeded to an elevator, where Massimo used a key to gain access. In the elevator, Rico held Tony in his arms, and Liz reached up to unzip her son's snowsuit jacket.

The doors silently opened onto an enormous foyer. A gold and crystal chandelier hung above a round, black, granite table. A cut crystal vase full of red and white roses was the only decoration. Lit wall sconces matched the chandelier.

Massimo led them to the living room, where a grand piano stood off to one side. Two large sofas faced each other with a square marble coffee table between. On either side were upholstered armchairs. "There are three bedrooms, each with its own bathing suite, a dining room, a library, and even a gym. I have taken the liberty of having the gourmet kitchen stocked."

"Good, and the other things?" Ricardo asked his PA.

"*Everything* is as you requested."

Anna grinned and said, "Tony, let us go see your room."

Tony took her hand and pulled her to the room Massimo had said was for him.

Liz and Ricardo followed. When Tony walked into the room, he squealed with joy. There were mountains of toys, and he went from one toy to the next. Jumping on to the giant black and white stuffed panda, he yelled, "Teddy."

Liz opened the walk-in closet to reveal more clothes than Tony could wear in a year.

Massimo said to Anna, "The room through the adjoining door is yours. The dress shop sent up a few items of clothing."

Liz went with Anna. Her mouth dropped when she opened the closet, then reached in to admire all the clothes hanging there. Her hand moved on her cheek, and she shook her head.

They returned to Tony's room. Massimo had left. Anna looked up at Ricardo and said, "*Grazie mille.*" A thousand thanks. She bent down to Tony. "Would you like me to play with you?"

"Come." Ricardo held Liz's elbow and led her to the master suite.

Her feet sank into the cream-colored Persian area rug. The room was dominated by a huge four-poster bed. What had caught her eye were three mannequins dressed in complete wedding attire.

"Choose one. The hotel is sending up a team from their salon. You *do* remember how I like your hair? The minister will arrive at seven this evening."

Liz stood there for a moment, not able to comprehend the situation. Confused, she tipped her head up to peer into his handsome face. "What exactly are you saying? What is it that you want?"

His voice sounded as smooth as honey, "Why, *cara mia*, you will be my wife, of course. Our son will have both a mother *and* a father. He will never again wonder who his father is." Then he thundered, "How could you keep him from me?"

Liz stretched her neck to stare into his fathomless eyes. *I kept him from you—you never wanted him or me.* "I don't want to marry you. Not now, not ever."

He grabbed her upper arms and pulled her into his hard body. "Little hypocrite. The way you kissed me; I know you wanted more of what we used to have together. I want our son to have both of us in his life, together as a family. If you do not want that, then be prepared. I will fight you for his custody, and you will see him only when I say so." He shook her. "Is that what you want?"

Tears welled in her eyes, and her throat tightened. She murmured, "No, that's not what I want."

A hot tear rolled down her cheek.

Rico dropped his hands to his sides. He briefly closed his eyes, then shook his head and leaned forward. "Get ready. I will send Tony in so you can explain that we are going to be a family."

"Ricardo…" Her voice broke. "I want us both to tell him. Please."

He smiled. "I will get him, *cara mia*."

Liz sat on the edge of the gold velvet divan at the foot of the four-poster bed. Her brain whirled. *He doesn't have to do more than say a word, and his demands are met. People jump to do his bidding—the toys, the clothes, even these gowns.* She gazed at the mannequins, the three dresses *were* beautiful. *Too bad none of them are mourning black.*

At precisely seven o'clock, Anna walked into the master bedroom. "Oh, you look beautiful," she said in her slight Italian accent.

"Look at you in that red cocktail dress," Liz said. "Your hair is styled so nice."

"Wait until you see Tony. Ricardo had a mini tuxedo ready for him."

Liz took a tremulous breath and smoothed the lace-embroidered fabric of her wedding gown. She glanced down at her dress. All three had been so pretty, she'd had a difficult time choosing, finally settling on this one, with its beaded neckline of sheer material continuing to the cap sleeves. The gown was fitted past the hips and then the skirt flared out as it reached the floor into a rounded train. The sheer and applique lace beaded with rhinestones scattered all over the dress and down the back; satin-covered buttons held the bodice together. *Is the demanding, insensitive bear out there?* "Is everything ready?"

"Yes, let us go into the living room. The minister is standing in front of the window. The drapes are open, and it is snowing. Everything looks so beautiful. Ricardo had a Christmas tree brought in and decorated while you were getting ready."

Liz heard the admiration in Anna's voice and almost rolled her eyes. Rico's charisma worked on women of all ages. Anna handed Liz a bouquet of red roses and opened the master bedroom door. As she took her first step toward Rico, the soft sound of a harp played the wedding march. Liz stopped herself from running out of the hotel and into the night, blizzard and all. She concentrated on breathing, too numb to do more than walk with Anna at her side.

Massimo stood next to Rico, both men in black tuxedos. Massimo had a red tie, while Rico and Tony both wore black bow ties. Tony stood next to his father holding a red satin pillow, his smile spread from ear to ear.

The ceremony was over all too quickly, and Anna took Tony to his bedroom. Massimo bid them good night.

Liz looked out the window at Central Park eighteen floors below. It was snowing harder now. A mix of big and small flakes fluttered and fell to the ground. The streetlamps cast a yellow glow over the sidewalk. She watched the headlights from one lone car as it drove by. She was alone with Rico, and *now* he was her husband. Her life had changed drastically, going from bad to worse in two days. How could she have let this happen? What would happen when he got tired of playing husband and daddy? Would he send another messenger to tell her and Tony that they had to go? He was moving on with someone else. What would she do then?

Ricardo's arms slipped around her waist. She stiffened.

"Rico, we only married for Tony's sake. It's not a real marriage. We—"

"Is that what you think?" His warm breath close to her ear sent shivers up her spine. "It is going to be a real marriage with a wedding night, a honeymoon, and… *everything*."

"But—"

He turned her in his powerful arms and bent his head, taking her mouth with his. Her hands came up to push at his chest, wiggling to get out of his embrace. He raised his head, and she looked into his eyes, then he brushed a kiss on her forehead and let her go. He went over to the gold champagne bucket, lifted the bottle, and popped the cork. He poured two glasses and brought one to her. Her hand trembled as she took the long-stemmed crystal flute.

He lifted his glass. "To my beautiful wife. We *will* make this marriage work."

He touched the rim of his glass to hers. The soft *clink* was the only sound in the room. Liz brought the glass to her lips and sipped the champagne. Rico's eyes burned into her soul. She turned away and placed her glass on the table next to the couch.

She found it difficult to believe that she was now Mrs. Ricardo Antonio DiMarco. He'd surprised her with an engagement ring and a diamond wedding band. She had over half a million dollars of diamonds on her finger, but to Rico, it was only money. Did it mean anything at all to him?

She'd been defiant in small ways. She'd asked the hairdresser to pin her hair up in an intricate chignon, no matter that he wanted her to wear it down around her shoulders. She looked up at Rico, who had a devilish glint in his eyes.

Liz picked up her champagne glass from the table. The pale liquid fizzed in the flute, and she drank a big gulp. She planned on staying as far away as possible from her new husband and the oversized bed that dominated the room.

RICARDO WATCHED Liz drink the champagne, noticing how she hesitated to be near him. He wasn't a man to force any woman against her will and especially not his wife. But oh, how he missed Liz. He pulled the right side of the bow and let the silk tie drape around his neck, then unbuttoned the top button of his shirt, followed by the next three buttons.

He ached for her. "More champagne?" He held the bottle up.

"Yes," she whispered.

Liz seemed reluctant to be in the same room with him. She held her glass out with trembling fingers. He saw the slight tremor and reached to steady her hand as he poured the liquid into her glass. *No man but I will ever touch you again. You are mine.*

"Thank you." She took a sip.

He shrugged out of his jacket and hung it over a chair, then toed off his shoes and pulled his socks off. *Thank you.* He was going to melt that formality of hers. He didn't want her to get drunk to escape him. He took the glass from her and put it on the table. He wrapped his arms around her tiny waist; she stiffened, unwilling to bend. He smiled to himself. *Challenge accepted.*

Rico took her mouth with gentle sweeps of his lips on her soft, sweet ones. He kissed down the satin smooth side of her neck, his open mouth drinking in her taste, feeling her pulse race under his lips. He stopped and ran his tongue along her collarbone. His hands moved down her back. It took an effort—as he opened every one of the tiny satin-covered buttons—not to rip the dress in his haste.

She stood on tiptoes while her hands slid along his arms up to his shoulders and met at the nape of his neck, her fingers making circles in his hair. Rico stroked her tongue with his and gently cajoled hers to spar with him. She gasped into his mouth when her gown pooled at her feet. He stood back and admired her curves, her skin creamy in the soft light. His hands reached for her waist and slid down to the gentle curve of her hips and around to her buttocks, his fingers spread, holding the soft flesh as he pulled her closer to the throb of his erection.

He lifted her to fit better against him while his lips

explored the soft texture of her neck, to her collarbone, and down over the swell of her breasts. The white lace of her bra prevented him from exploring her nipples.

His palms itched in his need to touch her. Rico unclasped the bra and slipped the satin straps down her arms. Her breasts fit perfectly in his hands. The nipples hard. He slowly bent his head. He *had* to feel the texture with his tongue. *I missed her.*

Rico held her close to him. He ran his tongue over the slope of her breast across the valley and up to her other nipple. Her fingers twined in his hair as she held his head against her breast, he sucked the taut nipple into his mouth. "Ahh." Her moan vibrated in his body, and his cock grew.

Lifting her in his arms, he carried her to the bed and laid her in the center… she was a temptress. Her luscious pink-tipped breasts quivered. His gaze traveled down her abdomen to the band of white lace on her thigh-high nylons that matched her lacy panties. Desire raced through his veins.

Rico unbuttoned the rest of his shirt. Liz moved from the center of the bed and crawled to him, kneeling on the mattress. She held his gaze and a sensuous light filled her emerald eyes as she unbuckled his belt. He laid her down again and followed her onto the cool sheets. The mass of her red-gold hair spread out on the pillows reminded him of waves of fire. His fingers slid through the silky softness of her hair—he kissed her throat and the tops of her breasts. One hand moved to her waist, so satiny soft, then across her abdomen. Liz moaned a long, deep sound.

Rico bent his head to her nipple and tongued the stiff peak, circled, and licked while his other hand moved further down and into the lace panties. One long finger sliding along the tuft of curls, he searched out her center—she was wet. He circled her bud, drenching it until she moaned again. That was his signal to slide her panties down her curvy legs. He slipped her sandals off along the way. He stopped to look at her glorious naked body. The triangle of tight red curls beckoned him. She *was* beautiful.

Rico looked at her, drinking in his fill of her siren's body—his erection had become almost painful as it pressed the fabric of his pants.

She averted her eyes, and her small hand crept down to cover herself. She was a contradiction to him… he knew the secrets of her soft flesh.

"You are lovely," he said huskily.

Slowly, she raised her emerald eyes to him, her lips parted, and she held his gaze.

She lay back into the pillows. He kissed her again. His tongue caressed her lips, tracing the contour before he sucked her delicate pink tongue into his mouth. His finger found her heat once more. She pushed his shirt open, and he stopped long enough to take it off, letting the shirt fall to the floor. She reached for his zipper. He growled as he unzipped his pants, shed them and his briefs in one motion.

Ricardo had wanted to go slow, but he knew he couldn't wait to be in her. He was determined to get his passion under control. He pulled her toward him, as she ran her fingers through the hair on his chest as he kissed her, and his hands moved down to caress the satin of her stomach.

He moved lower, and she murmured his name… He nudged her legs apart, and his tongue traced a path lower and lower, until his hands slid under her buttocks and lifted her to his hungry mouth. His tongue parted her, tasting her hot honey. Liz whimpered in his arms, her fingers tangled in his hair. She moaned when his thumbs parted the wet folds, his tongue slipping over and over her clit. Her fingers clenched and unclenched in his hair as she held him to her. When he sheathed his tongue in her, she arched into him.

"Oh, yesss, yes, oh Rico," she cried out and climaxed for him. He stayed with her, keeping his mouth and tongue where he knew she needed it most, right through her last shudder.

Rico rose up her lethal body. He throbbed at the entrance to her hot passage. "Look at me, Liz."

She opened her eyes. "Rico," his name left her lips on a sigh.

He entered her that first little bit; she was so tight. He wanted to thrust fully into her heat, sink into her, and have Liz take the pain of her betrayal away from him. With a will of steel, he got his passion under control. Slowly, an inch at a time, he let her get used to his size again.

Sweat broke out on his forehead. Liz wrapped her legs around his hips, bringing him further into her. With that move, she told him it was all right. He pushed into her again, pulling almost completely out before he thrust into her slick heat again and again.

Liz kept pace with him. Her moans turned into a scream that let him know, even before she stroked him in her hot core, that another orgasm had begun. Her body arched in his arms, and he watched as a pink flush spread from her chest into her cheeks.

Her eyes closed, and a smile spread across her sensuous lips as waves of pleasure washed over her. Rico held himself deep in her heat as he kissed her temple. Liz's contractions caressed him; clenching, she held him in her body. When her breathing returned to normal, she kissed his jaw and down his neck, across his shoulders. Liz lifted her legs higher, locking her ankles around his waist, sending him deeper into her heat.

He groaned and thrust into her—she coaxed him to his release as he pistoned into her tight core. She moaned and writhed under him. Rico gritted his teeth, threw his head back, and exploded into her, taking them both over the edge. She screamed his name, holding him deep in her quaking core.

His heart thudding, he stroked her hair from her flushed face, and he rolled onto his back, pulling her along with him. They lay together panting.

He hadn't felt this way in four years, not since the last time they were together. He had ached for her all that time. Ricardo hadn't realized how much—until now. Liz rolled off his body and sat against the pillows. He got out of bed and poured them more champagne.

She pulled the sheet up over her breasts, tucking it under her arms. Her cheeks were rosy, and her mass of red-gold hair mussed from his fingers, her lips kiss-swollen. He laughed to himself… She looked shy, even after the way she had abandoned herself to his lovemaking. God, he wanted her again. Her eyes widened—she'd seen his instant reaction to her. He was hard and ready for her again. He smiled down at her… she tried to shrink down on the bed.

He took the champagne glass from her fingers and placed it on the bedside table. She looked up at him, her eyes like saucers. He took her hand and placed a kiss on the center of her palm, then he pulled her along with him to the bathing suite. He turned on the shower and kissed her luscious mouth, soaping every inch of her curvy body.

He lifted her under the shower spray. "Wrap your legs around me."

A soft moan escaped her as she did what he said. His hands went under her buttocks, lifting her. In one stroke, he thrust into her and buried himself deep into her tight, hot heat. Her hands held his shoulders, her head fell back, allowing him access to her breasts. The nipples pink and puckered, inviting him to take them in his mouth, first one then the other. He brought them both to the edge, soaring higher, until together, they tumbled into ecstasy. He leaned her against the shower wall. They were breathless, and her legs slowly slid down from his hips to touch the tile floor. He shut off the shower, grabbed a towel from the heated rack, and dried her and then himself. She took a step to walk out of the shower.

"No wait," he said.

She stopped and looked at him. He bent and lifted her into his powerful arms, carrying her back to the bed. He laid her down and pulled the sheet to cover them. He wrapped his arms around her, and they fell asleep. He woke her again in the middle of the night and once more before dawn.

CHAPTER 6

The following morning, Rico woke up feeling better than he had in a long time. He could see out the bedroom suite window that it was still snowing. He held Liz's warm body in his arms. He had a son. Though there was much that Liz needed to explain, he knew he wouldn't trust her to be honest. He would have to learn to deal with her deceit and make sure she never cheated on him again. He would make her forget the other men she had been with.

He knew Tony was his son—the little boy looked just like him. He was still reeling from that knowledge. He wanted to know how Liz had ended up with an Italian friend that his son called *Nonna*, Grandma. Anna even spoke his Sicilian dialect. Oh, he had so many questions. He quietly got out of bed and pulled the comforter around his sleeping wife, then walked into the bathroom to shower and shave. He dressed in casual clothes.

Rico made his way through the living room to the kitchen, where he found Tony sitting at a table with Anna, having breakfast. Tony saw him and scooted off his chair, running into Rico's outstretched arms. "Papa, snow! Can we go out and play? *Nonna* said that Daddy in Italian is Papa. Am I Italian now?"

"Yes, you are. You are my son." He hugged the little boy to him, vowing to himself that he would make Liz pay for keeping his son from him. He put Tony back in his seat. Anna asked him if he wanted espresso and perhaps a roll. He sat at the table next to Tony. Over breakfast, Ricardo and Anna spoke in their native dialect. She told him how she and her husband had immigrated when they first married forty years ago. They had no more family in Sicily, and they had no children. When her husband passed away, she'd stayed in America. She thought of Liz as the daughter she never had and Tony as her grandson.

Ricardo turned as Tony ran into his mother's arms. Liz was in a white velvet hotel robe and barefoot, her hair loose and streaming down her back in silky curls, her face glowing. "Good morning, my darling. Did you sleep well?"

"Yes, Mama. Look, snow, can I go play? *Pleeease.*"

She smiled at him and ruffled his mop of black curls. "You have to get dressed first. Let's see what your father has planned for today."

She went to the fridge and poured herself a glass of orange juice. Standing with the door open, Liz drank the juice down. "Yummy, fresh squeezed." She poured another glass. "Tony, have you had your juice yet?"

He nodded. "Now can I go play?"

Liz smiled and put the full glass of juice on the table by her seat and went to pour herself a cup of coffee, not espresso, just regular American coffee. She picked a blueberry muffin from the pastry basket, placed it on a plate, and took a seat across from Tony. Anna sat next to Tony, and Rico was at the head of the table, a plate with a half-eaten roll from his breakfast and an espresso cup in front of him. Liz took a bite of her muffin, then another.

Tony chatted to the three adults. Rico answered his questions as best he could, not really knowing much about Iron Man or Spider-Man.

The ringing of Rico's cell phone interrupted their conversation. He glanced at the screen and said to Liz and Anna, "It's Massimo." Then he accepted the call. "Pronto. Si, si... va bene. Ciao."

RICARDO ENDED the call and turned back to Liz and Anna. "Massimo received word that the airports are closed indefinitely... We will have to occupy ourselves here. I am sure we can manage with Central Park across the street." He chuckled as he took a sip of his coffee.

Tony's head came up from the electronic tablet he held. "Park!"

"Why don't we wash your hands and brush your teeth, then we can put on one of your new outfits and go down to the park," Anna said.

Tony turned on his belly, sliding down the seat cushion, until his feet touched the floor, and scooted out of his chair, running toward his bedroom. Anna smiled and followed him.

Liz sat at the table, staring into her coffee cup. Rico thought of last night and how he felt that she'd held something back. Was she thinking of all the other men? Rico's jaw muscle tensed, and his lips thinned. He wouldn't let her think of anything but him ever again. The airport closure worked against him, but he would turn it to his advantage, the way he always did.

❧

LIZ, though deep in her own thoughts, knew that Rico watched her. She wouldn't let him see her distress. Her fear of the future with him. She'd agreed to the marriage only after he'd threatened her—he had the power to take Tony from her. She'd hoped for a celibate marriage, but last night had proved she was naive. She sipped her coffee while Rico sat across from her, expecting her to fall in line.

She didn't want to open old feelings—she preferred to let her hatred for Rico keep her going. He'd made love to her and in those moments, she'd abandoned her body to him. He had haunted her dreams; not one day had gone by when she didn't think of him or ache for him. Deep down, she kept a part of herself from him. She couldn't forget the past, no matter how much she bent to his will. Her body may respond, but her heart was frozen.

Liz mentally shook herself, but the memories flooded in, and she couldn't stop them washing over her. Four years ago, Rico, the handsome man at the table with her now, had destroyed her life, along with her love for him.

He'd gone on a business trip, promising to come home as soon as possible. She'd been so in love with him—they'd talked about marriage and how he wanted to take her to Sicily to meet his family.

What happened next had seemed so uncharacteristic for Rico, but what did Liz know at twenty-three? His aunt Angela ran his home in New York, and she'd tracked Liz down in the living room.

"I have something to tell you." Angela had wrung her hands as she spoke. "Ricardo called, and he told me that I am to let you know, you will have to pack your bags. He wants you out before he returns from his trip. I am sorry that I have to be the one to tell you this." Angela shook her head from side to side, sighed, and shrugged her shoulders. "This is not the first time I have to do this. It does not get easier, to see his, how you say? His woman of the moment asked to leave and never come back."

Liz had sat there, unable to comprehend what Angela was saying. With no chance for Liz to respond, Angela had taken her by the arm, patted her hand in a there, there, manner and said it would all work out, then led Liz to the bedroom.

Liz had snapped out of her daze when she saw the bed she and Rico had shared up until that very morning. Angela offered to help her pack, telling Liz that Ricardo didn't want her to take the clothing or the jewelry he'd bought her. She filled the suitcase from Angela with her meager collection of clothes hanging in the walk-in closet, leaving behind the many items of couture clothing he'd gifted her, along with all the furs and jewelry. Liz's throat had clogged with tears as she'd unclasped the diamond heart pendant, he'd given her on their six-month anniversary and placed it inside the wooden jewelry box with the carved yellow roses and hearts that adorned the top.

She had turned away; her body numb to all. She'd walked out of Rico's apartment and his life. As she'd ridden the elevator down to the ground floor, her thoughts jumbled. He said he loved her. They were going to get married. She caught herself on a sniffle—didn't she sound like a gullible, immature girl? Liz had stepped off the elevator with nowhere to go, no plan. She'd sat on a park bench in a daze. The next day, she'd wandered the streets of Manhattan trying to decide what to do. She had a college degree. Fully paid for with part of her parents' inheritance. She found a job and a temporary place to live in Brooklyn.

When she'd realized she was expecting, she tried to get in contact with Rico to let him know. Angela had said he'd moved on to a new mistress, but she would tell him that Liz had called. Days went by and no response, so Liz called again. Again, Angela answered the phone. "I'm sorry, Liz, but he will not talk to you. Yes, I tell him it was an urgent matter, but you know Ricardo."

Liz hadn't wanted to tell Angela what the urgent matter was, but Angela guessed. She told Liz that she would press Ricardo to see her, and she would, if Liz was okay with it, tell him of her circum-

stances. The following day, when Liz called, Angela asked to meet her downtown. At the appointment, Angela held Liz's hand and patted it and even shed a tear. "My nephew is not a nice man. I am sorry to say he did not care that you are expecting his child. He give me this for you." Angela had taken an envelope from her purse and put it on the table in front of Liz.

Liz looked at it, recognizing Rico's monogram. "What is this?"

Angela sounded sad. "I do not want to say what he say, but I will. He say, here give her this and tell her it is more than enough for an abortion."

That was when her love for Rico died, and her heart filled with hatred for him. Mortified, Liz had raised herself from the seat and on trembling legs, walked away from Angela, never looking back, leaving the envelope on the table.

Now, she sat at the same table as Rico. She shared his bed and was married to him, all for Tony, the baby he hadn't wanted. He had no *right* to be angry with her, he'd sent her away. Now, four years later, he'd changed his mind, just like that. She was supposed to be happy and trusting. Well, she didn't want *him*. She was doing this all for Tony. A little voice in her head laughed at her. *You're doing this because you're weak, and you missed him terribly.*

Tony ran into the kitchen with Anna close behind. "Mama, Papa, can I go play?"

He didn't wait for an answer but in his excitement, he ran and kissed his mother. He turned toward Rico and hesitated. Rico bent and picked Tony up, gave him a kiss on his chubby cheek, and told him to obey Anna.

CHAPTER 7

Once the elevator door closed with Anna and Tony going out to play in the snow, Ricardo rose and rounded the table to stand next to Liz's chair. He smoothed a curl of red silky hair behind her ear. She moved her head. Ricardo ignored that. "I'm sorry we can't have a proper honeymoon. It will have to wait."

She glanced up. "A honeymoon isn't necessary. You know—"

"Oh yes, it is, Liz. You see… you have to make me forget your deceit. You finished breakfast?"

She gestured to her empty plate. "You're stating the obvious, yet you're too blind to see that I've never been dishonest with you."

Ricardo drew her from the chair; she stood in front of him and turned away. "So, my dear sweet wife, that is how it is going to be." He pulled the slip knot on the satin belt of her robe while she remained unmoving. He put a finger under her chin, lifting her head.

"No."

He swooped down, capturing her mouth to prevent her

from saying anything else before he dragged her lethal body into his. She wouldn't move and kept her hands down at her sides, her lips clamped shut against him.

He released her lips and with both hands, grasped the lapels of the robe to spread the fabric apart. His body smoldered as he gazed at her naked skin. She visibly shivered and wouldn't look at him.

"Cold, *Cara?*" He pulled her into his arms. "Come, I will warm you." She stood firm, not moving.

He reached his hands to her waist, leaned forward, and lowered his voice, "Here on the kitchen table is good… or do you prefer standing in the middle—"

She jolted her head away. "No. Please, Anna and Tony… Rico."

"The bedroom?"

She lowered her head and with jerking motions, pulled the robe around her. Then she spun on her heel and with her head held high, walked through the living room, and down the hall to their bedroom.

His arousal pounded in his veins as he followed her. The robe clung to the curve of her back and with each step, her butt cheeks moved, enticing him. Knowing she was naked under the robe, in his present mood, he would have liked to take her against the wall in the kitchen. She was correct though, suppose Anna and Tony returned early. He followed Liz into the bedroom.

"Rico—"

He captured her mouth, crushing her body to his, demanding a response. He didn't care what she'd been about to say, he wanted to hear her moans of pleasure. He forced her lips open. He drove his tongue into her mouth. Dragging her against his body, he slipped the fabric off her shoulders. He kissed her neck and nipped at the tender flesh of her earlobe. "Feel how much I want you." He pressed her to him and slid the robe completely off so that it dropped to the floor around her bare feet. He lifted her into his arms and carried her to the bed. She groaned. He would turn her groans into screams of pleasure before he was done.

He kissed her lips, his mouth wild for her. He kissed her jaw, her neck, lingering on her pulse. He moved his hand down to a breast, his fingers teasing the tender bud until it became diamond hard. Her pulse raced under his lips, and he slowed his caresses. He sucked her left nipple into his mouth, and his hand moved lower over her belly, down to the tuft of red curls. She quivered beneath his hand.

He took his mouth from her nipple. "Spread your legs for me."

Her whimpered words were incomprehensible, his touch feather light over her mound. Her head was thrown back into the pillows, and streaks of red hair lay across the pillow and around her shoulders. He touched her lips with his, and she opened her mouth as she succumbed to his devouring kiss. He thrust his tongue into the sweet cavern of her mouth, and she lifted her hands to his shoulders.

One small hand stroked down from his shoulder to his arm, and she moved her legs. *Now you will be rewarded.* He slid his middle finger over her center, the curls damp. He pressed his finger into the seam until he was in to the first knuckle. "Ahh." She moaned against his mouth. He thrust his finger deeper into her. She was so wet, he thrust deeper into her vagina. He touched her clit with his thumb. She moaned into his mouth. Her knees lifted, offering more of her to his hand. He rubbed his thumb over her clit, knowing exactly what kind of pressure would drive her to an orgasm. She buried her face in his neck, kissing his shoulder, her hand pressing his to her. He smiled and then crooked his finger on her G-spot. Her imploring sounds becoming higher and higher as her hips lifted off the mattress. "Oh ahh, Rico." He waited for her last shudder to end before he unzipped his pants and threw them to the floor.

She opened her legs, and Rico placed his swollen, throbbing erection at her entrance. He thrust, and she lifted her hips. He was buried to the hilt in searing heat. He pulled out almost completely and plunged in again and again. She quaked and trembled around him, moving under him as she moaned her pleasure. She kissed across his chest, arching into him as he pistoned and ground into her. "Rico... Ric o o o...yes." She lifted her legs and wrapped them around his hips.

He groaned, "Cara mia, just a little more." Thrusting into her over and over, he raced toward a shuddering climax, shooting his hot seed into her. She clenched around him, holding him as she screamed her pleasure. Their panting breath mingled, and they were covered in a sheen of sweat.

Rico rolled over, taking Liz to lie against him. Holding her in his arms, he smoothed the silky mass of beautiful red hair from her flushed face. He couldn't stop touching her, running his hands along her velvet-soft skin. Their breathing returned to normal. Only moments ago, he had brought them both to ecstasy, such as he'd never known before. And yet, he wanted her again as if it were eons and not minutes since he'd been buried deep in her hot passage, loving her.

From the bed, they looked out the window as snow continued to fall, blanketing the city.

Rico picked Liz up and brought her over his body to straddle his hips. Her knees on either side, he lowered her onto his throbbing erection.

LIZ WAS AMAZED at how easily Rico maneuvered her onto him, and how ready she was to accept him. His arrogant, black-haired head moved forward, and his mouth lowered to one of her breasts. He sucked a nipple in, teasing it with his tongue until it was hard.

Her back arched, and her breasts lifted. As she did, she sunk further onto his steel-hard erection. His hands slid down to her hips. Fingers spread, he drew her close. His erotic skill drove her on. He plundered her mouth while he thrust up into her, holding her hips to fully embed himself into her.

She withered, arched her back, and brought her breasts—the nipples wet hard points from his hot mouth—to brush against the mat of his black chest hair, making her wild. She held back a moan as her pelvis tightened. He lifted and lowered her, and she pulsed around his steel-encased length. His hand snaked down her abdomen, trailing fire. A gasp escaped her and turned into moans of pleasure. She knew what he would do. She wanted all of this and didn't want it to end—he circled her throbbing clit with his finger. "Rico," she cried out as the spasms of her orgasm radiated through her in waves of pleasure. He covered her mouth with his in a searing kiss as he pumped into her. She tore her mouth away to scream, the pressure of his hands held her hips down as he thrust up into her. He shouted and hot spurts filled her as he came.

She fell forward on his massive chest, and he sank back into the pillows—both breathing heavy. There may have been a blizzard outside but in here, they were on the equator. She lay on his chest, her heart pounding in tempo with his. He felt *so* good in her. He smoothed her hair down her back, holding her. She nuzzled his neck, happy to be held in the circle of his arms, a place she thought never to be again. When he held her like this, she forgot that he had let her go. Though once she came back to earth, all the memories flooded back.

Liz disentangled herself from his long, powerful body, but Rico held her to his side. She pulled the sheet from the foot of the bed over them both—he let it fall to his waist while she kept it over her breasts and tucked the sheet around her.

His fingers stroked her arm. "Ah. A few more sessions like this, Liz, and you will make me forget the liar you are."

She stiffened. "You are the liar," she jerked herself out of his arms, "the one who plays games, the one who had me fired on a whim, not caring if I lived or starved. If—"

He pulled her toward him, and the sheet fell from her breasts. "Careful… what you say… *tesoro mio*, who you call a liar. I can still make your life hell."

He called her his treasure, made such passionate love to her, and then he continued to threaten her. She didn't want to live this way. "I never lied to you."

"No? What about your most recent deceit? How could you not let me know I had a son?"

For goodness sake, he threw me out. Doesn't he remember that? "I refuse to discuss this with you and—"

"Mama, Papa, where are you?" Liz and Ricardo just barely had time to cover up before their son burst into the room. He ran up to the bed, cheeks rosy, his heavy winter jacket unzipped, his mittens dangled off his hands, his snow pants, and boots on. Rico picked him up and put him on the bed with them.

"*Nonna* took me to the big park." Tony spread his arms wide to show them how big the park was.

"Did you play in the snow?" Rico asked.

"Yes, I made a snowman," he said, bouncing on the bed.

Liz laughed and held the sheet tight to her breasts. "Why don't you go to *Nonna*. Daddy and I will be right out."

"Okay." Tony scooted off the bed and ran out of the room.

Rico got out of bed. "I would offer to take a shower with

you." His black eyes roamed her body—she saw desire spark in the depths and the heat burned her. "But that would delay us, and Tony may come look for us again." He left to shower.

Liz was fuming mad at Rico. He threatened her and then made love to her. Anger knotted in her stomach. Standing tall, she walked into the dressing room. Half the closet was full of new clothes for her. Earlier, she had worn the hotel robe rather than clothes he provided. Now she had no choice but to wear them. She chose a red cashmere pullover sweater and paired it with cream-colored crepe slacks along with black suede high heels.

Liz walked into the living room where Anna and Tony sat on one of the long blue couches. Anna had dressed Tony in a new pair of denim jeans and a red plaid flannel shirt. He held a toy fire engine that he ran along the seat cushion, making the sound of a siren.

Rico, his hair damp from the shower, wore casual gray wool pants and a white shirt open at the neck. He walked into the living room, his cell phone to his ear. "*Si, grazie. Ciao.*" He ended the call and looked at Liz. "We have an update from this morning. The airport will be closed for at least another twenty-four hours."

She shrugged her shoulder. "Okay. I'm going to get lunch ready for Tony." What else was there to say? This only prolonged the dreaded honeymoon. She walked into the kitchen of the suite.

Ricardo came in. "Anna said he had a pretzel and part of a hot dog from a street vendor. He isn't hungry. I want to take him down to the lobby for a while."

Liz froze at his words, and her mouth dried. She worried that he would take her son and never come back. Would Rico really try to take Tony from her? She had done whatever he wanted. She'd get on her knees and beg him not to take Tony away if she had to. Her hand trembled as she touched it to her throat. "Why?" Her voice was a croak. "Where are you taking him?"

Ricardo's brow furrowed. "I was going to take him to the lobby. Anna said that carolers were preparing to sing around the Christmas tree."

Liz took a calming breath. "Oh, that will be fun. I will come—"

"No, *Tesoro*." He stepped closer and drew her into his powerful arms, kissing her temple. "This is father and son time."

She pulled away enough to raise her head and look up at him. He brought his sculpted lips down to brush hers in a soft kiss. His hands ran along her back and one cupped her buttock. Bringing her into his hard body, he pressed her so she could feel his arousal.

She gasped, and he squeezed her butt cheek. "We won't be long. Then Tony can take his nap. You and I will find some way to pass the time." Another brush of his lips on her temple, then he let her go and strode out of the kitchen to get Tony. Liz's heart pounded; he could make her forget her anger so easily. What had she become?

Liz made a cup of coffee for herself and one for Anna. She walked out of the kitchen and found Anna sitting in the living room, crocheting.

"I brought you a cup of coffee. Do you want anything more?" Liz placed the cup and saucer on the end table next to Anna.

"No, that is perfect."

Liz sat down on the chair facing her friend.

"Ricardo is a good man. He loves you. I can see that." Anna's fingers worked the hook and yarn into a square.

Liz shrugged and tilted her head to one side. "Well, you may think that, but I don't." She had never told anyone that

Ricardo had given her money to have an abortion. Her brain always shied away from that horrible thought.

She knew he couldn't possibly have loved her to suggest she rid herself of an innocent child. When they were together all those years ago, she thought he'd loved her but now the reality sank in. They'd shared something—lust.

"He married you right away, and he is going to be a good Papa to Tony, you wait and see."

"I won't stop him, but I will reserve judgment." She sipped her coffee.

"Look at what he did the minute he realized Tony was his son. I understand Italian, and the Sicilian dialect, and I know what Ricardo said to Massimo. He gave instructions for all the clothing, the toys, and even the wedding ceremony. *This.*" Anna put her crocheting on her lap and leaned forward with a shake of her head. "Is not something that a man would do without love for his family."

"We'll see."

The elevator door opened, and Tony ran in. Rico strode in after his son. Tony held a box of chocolates in his small hands and brought them over to Anna. "For you, *Nonna*, I picked them myself." He grinned.

"Oh, thank you." Anna took the box and kissed him on the cheek.

Rico held another box of chocolates, as well as two long boxes with thick red satin bows tied around each one. Tony brought the box of chocolates to his mother. She kissed him and then looked at Rico. He gave one of the long boxes to Anna and the other to Liz.

Anna lifted the lid off hers and exclaimed, "Oh, how beautiful. Not since my dear husband died has anyone given me chocolates and roses. *Grazie.*"

Liz smiled and then opened her box. "Oh." She glanced up to find Rico staring at her. In the box were two dozen yellow long-stem roses—he'd remembered that they were Liz's favorite color.

Anna said, "I see empty vases in the dining room next to the china. I go get two."

Liz followed her, and they put their roses into crystal vases. Liz brought hers into the bedroom and placed them on the table next to the bed. She rubbed one of the petals and inhaled the aroma of the fresh roses. Now it was time for Tony's nap. Liz prepared to take him to his room, but Anna said she would; she needed to rest as well. That left Ricardo and Liz alone in the living room.

Ricardo rubbed his furrowed brow, wondering what game Liz was up to—she looked truly uncomfortable. Earlier, she had shown genuine fear when all he'd wanted to do was take his son to the lobby. Now she acted distant, and her attitude toward him icy.

Well, he would melt that iceberg and turn her into a pool of lava. He would make sure she screamed in her pleasure before he finished. *What is going on with her? Why so hot in bed and so skittish out of bed?* Taking her hand, he said, "Let's sit on the sofa." She pulled her hand out of his and walked over to the accent chair instead. He didn't push the issue.

He decided to stand and face her. "Tonight, you and I will go to dinner in the hotel restaurant. I made a reservation for eight."

She shrugged with indifference.

"Liz, talk to me," he said with mounting frustration. "Tell me what is going on with you. If we are going to be a family, you need to be open with me."

Her lips thinned, and her eyes narrowed before she turned on him. "Oh really? I'm the one that must be open with you, but you can continue to keep your dirty secrets, calling *me* a liar. You pretend nothing happened before." She shook her head of red hair, her face flushed. "Now after all these years, just because for whatever reason the *powerful* Ricardo DiMarco has, you want us to be a family. Well, I—"

She seemed genuinely angry—what an actress. He'd had enough. "Careful what you say. I know what kind of a, a slut you are. You spread your legs for any man with money, little gold digger."

The photos he had of her with Andre and all those other men fed the rage that wound through his belly. She would pay for her lies. Nothing short of her on her knees, begging him to keep her and not take Tony away would satisfy him.

He grabbed her arm and dragged her out of the chair. She tugged free. "Don't." That one word provoked him. He sat with her on the sofa. What would he do with her? The only time he acted on impulse was with her. In business and in any other part of his life, he could think rationally, walk away from a deal that didn't profit him. He gritted his teeth and held her around the waist, lifting her onto his lap. She moved, and the hardness of his arousal pressed into her hip.

"No." Her voice sounded panicky.

He kissed her parted lips.

"Mmm… mmm." Panting, she moved her head away from him, her lips inches from his. "If you think I'm such a slut," pant, pant, "and not fit to be with you, why did you marry me? Why didn't you make me sign a prenuptial—"

He tightened his hold.

She stopped talking.

His eyes roamed her flushed face and then down her lethal body. Her sweater had ridden up, leaving the satin smooth skin of her midriff bare. Her breasts heaved.

"Be careful what you say—I can still take *my son* from you, and you will only see him when *I* say you may."

Liz instantly stopped struggling. Her eyes widened, and her mouth opened in horror at his words. She fell to her knees between his legs, her hand on his thigh. A tear rolled down her cheek.

"Do you want me to beg you?" She wiped at her cheek with the back of her hand. "Well, then I will. Please, please, Rico, don't take him from me. I *know* you can."

At the anguish in her voice, he groaned. "No, *cara mia*, get up." Whatever she'd been, he knew she was a good and loving mother.

He leaned forward, his hands on her upper arms, and lifted her so that she stood before him. He rose and held her in his arms, pulling her soft body into his.

She looked up at him; a tear clung to her cheek. He held her face in his hands and wiped the tears away with his thumbs. He kissed away the one that rolled down her delicate cheek.

"Oh, *cara mia*, I never meant for you to be upset." He lifted her in his arms. He was grateful that she didn't fight him as he carried her into their bedroom. Rico locked the door. "Just in case Tony comes looking for us."

He stood her by the bed as his hands slid up her waist. He kissed her temple, her eyes, and then her lips. He slipped off her sweater to reveal a sexy red lace bra. The sheer cups barely covered her breasts. Her nipples were hard buds pointing through the delicate see-through fabric.

"You are beautiful." He bent his head to kiss her through the fabric. She didn't object. Encouraged by that, he unhooked her bra, dropping kisses over her breasts and in the valley between. He traced one extended nipple with his tongue, drawing it into his mouth. He held her other breast, taking the bud between his forefinger and thumb, applying enough pressure to make her moan. He licked her nipples over and over again. She arched into him, and they fell onto the satin coverlet of the bed.

He unzipped her cream-colored slacks; as he slid them

down, he kissed her belly. Sliding the pants down her legs, he dropped the fabric to the floor. He moved over her lethal body. Her hair was a mass of red waves across the pillow and he spread her satin-smooth curvy legs with his knee.

"*Abracia me*, put your arms around me."

She did. Her lids shut as she reached her arms up to slide around his neck.

He lowered his mouth, and her lips opened in anticipation. He brushed his lips in feather-light touches across hers. Her fingers moved on the nape of his neck. He slipped his tongue into her mouth to stroke hers once, twice. She sucked on his, and molten heat settled in his groin. He left her hot mouth to kiss along her jaw to the curve of her throat. Her pulse raced under his lips, and he stopped to lick the hollow at the base of her throat and along her collarbone.

He knew how she loved that. His hand teased her breast, plucking the excited nipple until she moved, nudging him to her other breast. He took what she offered, opening his mouth to suck the pointed nipple in and using his tongue to drive her crazy.

The sound of her moan was music to his ears. His other hand moved down her abdomen and traced a path to the top of the red thong. Back up to her belly and oh-so-slow down to the thong.

He would make her beg. He felt the tightness in her abdomen as his hand stroked her soft skin. His hand moved further down, and the tips of his fingers brushed past the elastic band of the red thong. She quivered, and her thighs trembled.

"Oh…" she moaned as the tension left her legs, in an invitation for him to go further sln his exploration.

He lifted his head from her nipple and rising, kissed her lips. He slid his tongue into her sweet mouth and tasted her surrender.

She whimpered when he ignored what she wanted. He gazed into her eyes. His hand remained on her mound, without moving. He watched her as she bit her bottom lip. Her eyes fluttered closed. She groaned and then lifted her buttocks ever so slightly, undulating her hips. "Rico…"

He sucked the pout of her bottom lip into his mouth and continued to tease her, just out of reach of where he knew she wanted his touch… his fingers in the tight curls, at the seam of her entrance. He thrust his tongue into her sweet mouth just as his middle finger entered her. She drenched his finger. His dick swelled, and he strove for control.

His thumb moved back and forth, back, and forth on the bud of nerves and with each stroke, he applied more pressure. She was so wet. He would make her come. She whimpered into his mouth and sucked his tongue. Her hips lifted. Ricardo knew how to make her wild, so he moved down her body.

"Oh, God," she moaned when he stopped to slide her thong off. He couldn't hold back the smile that crossed his lips.

He dipped his tongue into her belly button. Spreading her legs with his knees, he kissed, lower and lower. His hands led the way, opening her to his mouth. The tip of his tongue pressed her clit, then sliding over and around the base.

"Rico."

He sucked it into his mouth. She let out a long moan, and her hips lifted, opening herself to his mouth. He licked and sucked then thrust his tongue into her sweet honey. He kept her at that intensity, and her fingers dug in his hair.

Licking, going deeper into her hot sweetness.

She moaned, "Oh, please." Her fingers tangled in his hair. He shifted his hands under her, holding the two globes of her buttocks. His shoulders wedged between her thighs. He kept her still as he thrust his tongue deeper and deeper into her vagina.

"Rico… Oh… I… I… ahh," she whimpered.

The shudders of her climax tasted so good on his tongue.

He slid up her siren's body and covered her mouth with his, absorbing her moans of pleasure. He'd had no time to undress, he needed her that much. He unzipped his pants and thrust into her heat. He lifted her legs over his shoulders. He had to be in her hot, oh so tight body. He wanted to feel her orgasm around him. He ached with his need. He pushed her to another orgasm.

"Rico, I can't…"

He thrust. "*Si.*" Buried deep in her heat, he moved his hips from side to side. "You can."

Liz moaned, "Yes… yes, oh."

"Liz…" He groaned and couldn't help himself. He gritted his teeth as his cock pulsed in her heat, and he fought the urge to explode into her. Then her body shuddered, clenching him in her, and he growled with pleasure as he erupted into her core.

He held her against his side in the afterglow and skimmed his fingers through her hair. When their breathing returned to normal, he said, "I am sorry if I rushed you. I just had to be in you. I couldn't wait."

She didn't answer. They heard Tony running down the hall. "You go take your shower, and I will take care of our son." Ricardo kissed her lightly on the lips just before she slipped into the bathroom.

CHAPTER 8

That night, Rico took Liz to the restaurant at their hotel. The snow had finally stopped. Rico hoped they would be able to fly out sometime tomorrow. At first, he'd planned on a honeymoon for them, but now with this delay, he just wanted to get home to Sicily. He would discuss this with Liz over dinner.

Her burgundy velvet dress clung to her curves, and the hem ended halfway between her knees and her thighs. She wore nude nylons and black stiletto heels. The diamond earrings he had given her earlier peeked through the mass of red-gold hair around her heart-shaped face, curling down past her breasts. With a touch of color on her lips, she picked up her wine glass, and the diamonds on her left hand sparkled in the candlelight.

"I know I promised you a honeymoon, but we will have to postpone it until later in the year. I want to get home to Palermo as soon as possible. I have left Gianni babysitting all the relatives so that we can take the jet and fly back as soon as we get clearance from JFK."

She looked up at him, her eyes round. "Palermo? But I... I thought you lived here in New York?"

He reached for her hand. "*Si, cara mia*. I have the penthouse on the Upper East Side, but Palermo has been my home for the last two years. Since my father had a heart attack." He held her small hand in his and gave her a comforting squeeze. "Tony will love it. He will have his grandparents, aunts, uncles, and cousins."

Liz swallowed past the lump that formed in her throat, her thoughts running in all directions in her head. How could she live in a foreign country with a man who only a few hours ago had called her a liar and more? Then made love to her as if she were his greatest treasure.

What about her? Giving in to him so easily and taking all he had to offer. She was grateful he wanted to be a father to Tony, and a husband to her. But what kind of husband? The shameful way he spoke to her and then her falling into his bed with just a snap of his fingers. With all that, she hated him, though not a day had gone by that she hadn't thought of him, his lovemaking.

She had missed him more than she was willing to admit. Now he would take her away from the only place she knew and move halfway around the world to a place where she didn't understand the language or the customs.

Rico rubbed the inside of her wrist with his thumb. "Do not worry. Anna will come with us, and she can help you learn the language. My mother and father both speak English, so do Gianni and Sofia. We will all be living near each other. They'll help you and Tony adapt."

She shuddered inwardly and managed a tremulous smile.

Her appetite gone, she focused on his large hand caressing hers, offering comfort.

"Come, let us go to the Grand Ballroom." He held her hand, their fingers woven together as they strolled down the large corridor. A row of eight-foot-tall Christmas trees, decorated with red and gold baubles, lined the way. Between the trees, vases of fresh red and white flowers stood on marble pedestals. An orchestra, with the women dressed in black gowns, and the men dressed in tuxedos, played for the guests that had been snowed in. Ricardo took her in his arms as the music began.

"Do you remember the first time we danced the waltz?"

She smiled. "Our first date after the cruise."

"You wore a black cocktail dress."

She laughed. "You taught me the steps right there on the dance floor."

They stayed out until late, dancing and drinking champagne, then he took her back to their suite. Looking in on Tony, who slept like an angel, they tiptoed out of his room, gently closing the door. Rico bent and lifted Liz in his arms. Her gasp of surprise caught in her throat. She wrapped her arms around his neck, nestled her head on his shoulder, and closed her eyes, thinking how handsome he looked in his tuxedo.

In their room, he moved his arm from under her knees and let her legs dangle down his body. Her arms wrapped tighter around his neck, his big powerful hands moved to her buttocks, lifting her higher against him. She held onto his shoulders and gazed into his eyes, the flame of desire warming her.

Liz bent her head down to his sculpted lips, her mouth pressed against his. Her breasts swelled in the confinement of her dress and bra. Her body slid down his as he turned to lock the door—then he reached around, taking her lips again, the sound of her zipper sliding down the back of her dress drowned out by the beat of her heart. She untied his bow tie with trembling fingers, then reached for the buttons of his white silk shirt.

Her dress pooled around her feet. He brushed her hands away from his shirt. She looked into his eyes, and he kissed her hands, first one then the other. He flashed a brilliant smile, and in one move, ripped his shirt open and off, taking her back into his arms.

"Bella," he said before his mouth covered hers, caressing her lips with soft sweeps. He unhooked her bra and stopped her when she reached for the zipper of his pants—she'd felt his erection against her while they danced in the ballroom. He took her nipple into his mouth and ran his tongue around the stiff peak. She sighed as it drew tighter, then he moved on to the other, doing the same.

He knelt and rolled her stockings down and off her legs, his hands sliding up the backs of her thighs, while his black, passion-filled eyes burned into her. He pulled the globes of her buttocks forward, and his tongue dipped into her navel. She couldn't stop the moan as his tongue glided over her flesh to the elastic of her panties. He teased her with his tongue and lips, and she shivered as he lowered the lace of her panties to her ankles.

"Hold my shoulders."

Heat spread through her at his words. He lifted one foot out of the panties, then lifted her other foot and guided it so she stood with her feet apart. His hands spread fire as they skimmed up the back of her legs. He kissed her abdomen, and she trembled; his hands massaged her buttocks. He spread hot kisses along her abdomen, his hands moved around to her hips. She moaned when his thumbs met at the juncture of her legs. Rico moved his thumbs, and heat spread lower just as his hands exposed her to the thrust of his tongue into her center. Her hands lifted from his shoulders, and her fingers tangled in his thick hair.

Liz was on fire—heat sizzled through her veins. Rico drove her crazy with each thrust of his oh-so-great tongue into her vagina. Then he added one of his long fingers. She loved the way his tongue circled her sensitive clit. She tried to hold back a moan as he inserted another finger inside her, his tongue never leaving her, increasing her pleasure. When he thrust his fingers in and out of her, she didn't know how much more she could take.

Her hands cupped his head, her fingers in his hair clenching, holding him closer to her center. He touched her knee and lifted her leg so that her upper thigh rested on his broad shoulder. He kissed her inner thigh.

"Rico," she whimpered when his fingers left her, and he dragged his tongue to swirl her clit. "Ah," she moaned and massaged his head. He pulled her forward, and she eagerly pressed herself to him, needing what he did to her. Her abdomen tightened, a coil of fire in her core pulsed with the delicious sensation his masterful tongue gave her. She held his head, her thigh on his shoulder, and her lower leg wrapped firmly around him she abandoned herself to the waves of her glorious climax.

Ecstasy… His knowing tongue stayed where she needed him as he held her body up, her pleasure intense.

When her breathing almost returned to normal, he replaced his tongue with his finger. Liz sighed, her brain sluggish in her thoughts—oh, he wasn't done yet. The slow movement of his long finger searching, she held his head to her, waiting. "Please, I…" she moaned, her thigh on his shoulder and his hand on her buttock held her up. His tongue on her clit brought more pleasure as he crooked his finger, and the walls of her vagina pulsed.

"Rico." Her head fell back. "Oh, so very good."

His mouth was demanding as he sucked on her clitoris His finger rubbed her G-spot. Her hips undulated, wild in her need. She couldn't hold back the scream as the waves of her orgasm radiated through her body.

Euphoria, "Rico." Her eyes closed. The next thing Liz knew, she lay in the center of the bed. Rico had removed the rest of his clothing. "What happened?" Had she fainted?

Rico bent and kissed her mouth. "You make me crazy. *La Petite Mort*, you never experienced that before." He kissed her harder. She ran her tongue along his, and her hand slid up and down his back. He sucked her nipples. His erection brushed her thigh as he nudged her legs apart.

Then for the first time since they got back together, Liz moved her hand down between their bodies to hold his huge erection, and her thumb glided along the tip of his pulsing head before she guided him into her body.

He groaned.

"Oh Liz, I have missed you," he whispered against her lips. Thrust after thrust, he buried himself fully into her, and she was going to come again.

Her legs wrapped around his waist. Her breasts arched into his chest. He shuddered into her once, twice, and a final time.

Liz panted… his weight felt so good, blanketing her. She knew he held most of his weight off her, but she loved this moment after they'd both orgasmed. She kissed his jaw and almost sighed. The feel of him still in her and over her was bliss.

He rolled to his side, bringing her along to lie on top of his massive chest. His hands slid along her back, over the curve of her buttocks—he squeezed one globe. She looked at him, her eyes half-closed, with a smile on her lips. Her heart melted.

Then he ruined it.

In his deep, sensual tones he said, "Ah, Liz, these sessions will help me to forget your lies." He smoothed her hair from her face and lifted her chin to stare into her eyes. "You ask me why I didn't make you sign a prenuptial agreement. Well, now you know. I do not need one. I will never give you a divorce. I will keep you satisfied." His voice hardened. "You will never be with anyone but me ever again!" He shook her. "Only me."

His words sank into her muddled brain. She tried to pull out of his strong arms to get off his hard body.

He held her a moment longer. "You know your struggles will not stop me."

She knew.

He released her. She pulled up the covers from the foot of the bed, moving as far from him as she could get. He rolled to his side, propped his head on his hand, and laughed. She bristled at the sound of his laughter and rolled away from him. Oh, she was furious— how could she forget what an uncaring, callous man he really was? He pulled her toward him.

"Don't. I won't let you touch me again." Her voice broke.

He laughed. "I only want to hold you, but if I wanted you again… you would. Perhaps next time I *will* make you beg me."

She cringed because she knew he could make her beg, and she would beg him.

She hated him.

She hated herself even more. She kept her back to him, stiff with tension, and wouldn't let him hear her cry as hot tears slid down her cheeks.

Ricardo pushed himself up against the upholstered headboard of the bed in the hotel suite, unhappy with himself. He had baited Liz too much, and now her body shook with silent tears. He stopped himself from caressing her hair and trying to make her feel better, but barely. The moonlight streaming through the window silvered her body. She was beautiful *and* his forever. No other man would ever touch her again. She finally fell asleep. He curled himself around her and slept as well, holding Liz to him.

In the morning, he left her sleeping in the bed. He showered and dressed, then called Massimo. He wanted an update on departure times. The airport was set to open at noon, but there were commercial as well as other private jets ahead of them. Massimo made some phone calls, but they wouldn't be cleared for takeoff until that night.

"Were you able to reach the judge? Did you take care of the birth certificate and passports?" he said into the phone.

"Yes."

With the city shut down, Massimo had pulled some strings to secure passports for Liz, Tony, and Anna. Liz, upset from the previous night, hadn't spoken a word to Ricardo. Now they sat in the suite's theater and watched one of Tony's favorite movies. Hotel staff moved around the suite and packed their belongings.

LIZ DIDN'T KNOW what to expect, especially with Rico's attitude toward her. He showed her how weak she was when it came to him. Her hedonistic side took over, and the smart, level-headed woman vanished in the sexual haze from her husband's body.

Where would they live? How would Tony react to living in a foreign country, not really knowing the language? Yes, they both had Anna, but it was a scary endeavor for her little boy *and* her.

Rico had told her that the rest of the family would be staying in New York City a few more days, then flying out with Gianni and Sofia. That would give Rico a chance to introduce her and Tony to his parents.

She wished she could hold back time, but before long, they entered the limousine for the drive to the airport. She and Anna both had new coats, leather wool-lined gloves, and fur hats. Snow blanketed New York City and the red, blue, green, and yellow Christmas lights made it appear enchanted. Liz looked out the limo's window and tried not to let Tony see her sadness.

The jet waited by the private hangar belonging to DiMarco Enterprises. Massimo had gotten out of the stretch limousine first and gone ahead. Liz and Anna climbed the steps in front of Rico, who carried Tony to board the plane. The pilot and co-pilot along with three flight attendants greeted them. The cream and navy-blue interior was as luxurious as Liz remembered, with thick, plush carpet throughout. There were two private sleeping suites on board, one larger than the other. Another area of the cabin had seats that reclined into beds. Luxury and privacy at every turn. Ricardo even had an office on board with a couch that turned into a *very* comfortable bed.

Rico, Liz, and Tony took seats at the front of the cabin. Rico strapped Tony in next to Liz, then he checked Liz's seatbelt, before settling on the other side of Tony. Massimo and Anna continued the Sicilian conversation they'd begun in the limousine, heads together nearby. Rico whispered to Liz, "Massimo and Anna are talking in the Sicilian dialect. They are reminiscing about places Anna knew in her younger days."

Rico tried not to listen and turned his attention to Tony and Liz. He took her small hand, stroking her wrist with his thumb. Liz was fearful of flying, and he had always held her hand when they took off and landed. A grin crossed his lips, remembering how several times he had made use of the bedroom, and even his office couch, so that she would forget her fears. Now, with *company* on board, as well as his son, he just held her hand.

Liz looked up at him. He smiled and didn't let go of her hand, not until the plane reached cruising altitude. Once it was announced that they could unbuckle their seatbelts, Tony wanted to explore the plane. The pilot came out and took him into the cockpit. Ricardo leaned over and gently kissed Liz on the lips.

"We will be having dinner shortly. Come, *cara mia*, relax." He held her close for a moment. "I will always take care of you and Tony."

It was early morning when they landed at the airport in Palermo. A car waited on the tarmac to transport them from Punta Raisi to his home. The twenty-minute ride was mostly in silence as Tony slept in his car seat. Rico took them to his house while Massimo went to the office. He wanted to get Liz and Tony settled after the long flight before he took them to meet his parents. It would be a surprise for his family to find out he had a wife, but to see that he had a three-and-a-half-year-old son... well, that might be a shock No one other than his parents would dare to question him.

They exited the highway and turned down a wide avenue. There wasn't too much traffic at this early hour, and Liz peered out the window. The scenery changed to narrow tree-lined streets and finally, they arrived before a three-story structure of honey-colored stone with baroque balconies along the front that he called home.

Ricardo's housekeeper Rosaria opened the double doors for them. She had a huge smile on her wrinkled face when she saw Tony. "This house needs children," she said in Italian.

Rosaria showed Anna her new room, while Ricardo took Liz and Tony to the nursery, not far from Anna's—a cozy living room separated the two bedrooms. "There are another four bedrooms on this floor," Rico said before he led Liz to the steps.

"Where are we going?"

"Up to the third floor. That is where the master suite is."

She stopped short. "On a different floor from Tony?"

"Yes, that is the way the house is set up. Tony will have Anna near, and we can be at his side in a moment if he needs us."

He led her up the marble steps. The entire third floor was the master suite. They walked into the master bedroom. Liz glanced up at the domed ceiling, with its fresco of clouds and blue skies above the huge bed. From the center hung an antique crystal chandelier. Liz glimpsed at the magnificent view of the Mediterranean Sea from the wall of ceiling-to-floor windows.

She was still angry with Rico—the way he had treated her

their last night in New York City. Then to make matters worse, during the flight, he'd handed out their new passports. He showed Liz hers with her new name, Elizabeth DiMarco. She'd expected that, but when she saw Tony's passport, her anger mounted. Antonio Giuseppe DiMarco, was printed on her son's.

"His name is Tony Ferguson. That is what his birth certificate says." She'd tried to keep her voice low, but Rico tested her patience.

"Not anymore. I had it corrected. He is a DiMarco, and his name is Antonio Giuseppe DiMarco."

He never raised his voice at her but showed his displeasure in other ways. She knew he would make her pay for not giving Tony his paternal grandfather's name. How could she have? Why would she? Rico had left her to her own means—he'd had his messenger tell her to leave his home. He'd had Angela deliver an envelope with cash for an abortion.

Now, he just took it upon himself to change *her* son's name. What would prevent him from cutting her out of his life again? His comment about the prenuptial, the way he threw her weakness for him in her face. He would never give her a divorce. She felt trapped. He would keep Tony and not let her see her son. He had the wealth and the power to get what he wanted. Oh, how she hated him at times like this, with his arrogant male dominance.

She did little things in her own way to needle him. Like the way she'd styled her hair for her wedding, swept up, knowing he wanted her hair down around her shoulders. Now she always wore it up during the day; it made her look sophisticated. He wanted her to sit next to him, so she always found a seat far from him. The last time she'd done that though, he'd risen from his chair, picked her up, then sat down, and pulled her onto his lap. They'd been alone, and his big hands had roamed all over her body. Before she knew it, she had melted in his embrace.

He cleared his throat, bringing her out of her thoughts. "We will go to my parents' house for *pranzo*, lunch. Anna said she will join us. I will get our son and meet you downstairs."

"I'm ready." She walked out of their room and down the stairs. Tony sat in the middle of his room, surrounded by toys. He had more than enough toys for ten boys to play with and never get tired. She shook her head. *A few days ago, I didn't know how I would buy him just one toy, and his father buys him all this.*

"Come, we are going to meet your other *Nonna* and *Nonno*, your grandfather." Rico hunkered down by his son. "Would you like to bring some toys with you?"

"Can I bring my trains?"

"Well, that set is too big. How about the police car and the fire truck?"

"Okay." Tony jumped up and went to get the toys his father had suggested.

They met Anna in the main living room on the first floor. The four of them got into Rico's BMW. Once they turned off the lane the palazzo was on, the traffic intensified. Not even Manhattan traffic could've prepared Liz for this chaos, with cars going in all directions at the same time, pedestrians crossing right into the traffic, bicyclists cutting cars off. The short drive to Rico's parents' home was an eye opener for Liz.

Rico stopped the car in front of a sprawling villa. "This is our ancestral home; it has been in the DiMarco family for many generations."

Liz's stomach tightened with worry. Even though Rico told her he'd called his parents this morning preparing them with the news of his marriage and son, she was concerned. *What if they don't like Tony?* The front door opened, and

Rico's mother, a petite woman with hair the color of wheat, kissed Ricardo and then turned to Liz.

"Please come in. I am happy to meet you." The elder DiMarcos were gracious and welcomed her to the family, kissing her on both cheeks—the traditional Italian greeting. Their lovely home had all the modern conveniences mixed with the traditional within the original structure of the house.

Liz saw how they fell in love with Tony, though they called him Antonio. Rico's mother was delighted to find Anna spoke Italian and that she was a dear friend to Liz. Lunch was more a five-course dinner, served by their cook. They teased Liz that she would have to get used to eating a large meal during the day and a smaller one in the evening. Liz was grateful that Rico stayed near her, but his parents were so welcoming and immediately made her feel like one of the family.

Once home, Rico informed her that he had to go out, and she shouldn't hold supper for him. The palazzo was big and so empty without him. What would she do to make the time go by? She and Anna talked while Tony played with his toys. They were all tired, so Anna voted for sleep. Liz gave Tony his bath and read him a bedtime story. With them both out, Liz felt alone in this enormous house.

Climbing the marble steps to the third-level master bedroom, Liz walked into the bathing suite, turned on the water, and filled the round sunken tub in the center of the heated marble floor. Once filled, she turned on the jets and stepped down into the warm, swirling water. A good soak would help her relax, and then she would get into bed with a book to read. *Where was Rico? Would he always just go out and leave me home alone?*

She was in bed with a book on her lap when she heard him come up the stairs. He leaned against the door frame.

"Ah, my beautiful, faithless wife. The woman who kept my son from me. All prim and proper. Waiting for your husband?" His accent was heavy. He strode into the room and closed the door behind him.

He's drunk. Ricardo never drank to excess, so this left her stunned. He was always in control. Drinking caused mistakes and loss of control, which he would never allow. *This is new.* She settled back against the pillows. She didn't know how to deal with a drunk Rico.

He loosened his tie, slipped out of his Italian leather loafers, and threw the tie onto the floor. By the time he reached the foot of the bed, all he had on were his pants. He came around to her side of the bed. She held her breath as he reached for her. He held her by her upper arms and pulled her to the edge of the mattress. Even on her knees, she had to tilt her head up to look into his coal-black eyes.

Gold flecks burned in the depths, "Ah, *bella*. Do you know how beautiful you are?"

His eyes roamed over her body covered in a blue satin nightgown.

"Do you know how you drive me crazy?" He bent and took her mouth with his.

The taste of brandy on his tongue wasn't repugnant. *He wasn't drunk. He may have only had one drink.* He was angry with her, that she could tell by the way he pulled her against him. His big, strong hands ran down her back as he pressed her against him and made her feel how hard he was. She pushed against his bare chest with her hands. He ignored the pressure and smiled; one ebony brow rose. He bent his head to suck her nipple through the fabric of the nightgown. She tried to squirm away from him, but he wasn't having any of that. He stepped back from her just long enough to pull the negligée up over her head.

~

RICARDO LOOKED AT LIZ, naked on her knees at the edge of the mattress. *God, she is beautiful.* Why did he think he could be with his mistress when he had Liz in his bed waiting for him? Rico wouldn't force her. He would never do that to a woman and especially not his wife, but he would make her want him as much as he ached to be buried in her molten heat.

He fondled her breast, kissed the underside and the valley between, then his tongue traced a path over the other breast and tongued the nipple. His other hand roamed along her backside, over the curve of her silken buttocks then down the back of her thigh. Both hands moved lower, to just above the back of her bent knees. She wiggled and pushed at his chest, but Rico slid his hands between her knees and parted them, spreading her. She moved forward to escape his hands, but that just brought her in contact with his erection, now bursting to be out of his pants. She gasped and threw her hips back. He grinned, prepared for that move. His finger slid into her heat.

The little liar wanted him. She drenched his finger with her desire. He would make her beg. At this angle, he could reach all the wet, sensitive parts of her. She couldn't escape his touch. Her head fell back, he took her parted lips, and his tongue traced the full lower lip, while his finger moved from her clitoris into her center. He added a second finger when she moved her hips forward to get away. He thrust his tongue into her open mouth, sucked her lower lip into his mouth while his fingers moved from her hot center to her bundle of nerves and back again.

He recognized the moment she wanted what he did to go on. In her desire, she rolled her hips to catch his fingers in her hot, wet center.

She arched her back, and her breasts pressed against his chest; her nipples were hard. Her head fell back, her hands went to his shoulders, her eyes were closed, the beginning of a smile on her sensuous lips. He bent to take a nipple into his mouth. She sucked in her breath.

He knew she was close to climax, so he stopped. She groaned, and she tried to follow his fingers. He kept them just out of reach.

"Open your eyes," he rasped the command.

She did, and the emerald color of those cat eyes blazed at him.

"Oh, Liz, you are exquisite."

He started again, just one finger in her center, and slid the tip along to her clit. Her knees spread wider as she tried to lower herself onto his finger. He moved his finger forward, she followed. Her luscious body was so tight against his erection, he didn't know if he could continue this game he had started. He may well be the one who begged. She felt so good and hot. He would stop this and just take her.

Liz held his shoulders, her nails digging in. He leaned over and covered her mouth, and his tongue slid between her parted lips at the same time his finger circled her hard bud. She moaned into his mouth, her knees spread wider, and he thrust into her center and then forward, pressing the bud, moving his finger from side to side. He plucked and teased her clit. Small panting sounds escaped her lips. He slid his finger back into her center, adding another. She pulled her mouth away from his to suck in air. He stopped.

"Rico." She sobbed and reached down to unbutton his pants. He laughed. His throbbing erection pressed against her abdomen.

She slid his pants and underwear down the hard muscles of his legs. He bent and took her mouth as he stepped out of his pants. She sucked his tongue, and he found her moving his fingers slowly, and then so deep into her center. Panting, she whimpered, "Please, Rico. Please… make me… come."

Ah, the words he wanted to hear.

"*Si.*"

He bent his knees, braced his legs, and lifted her off the bed and onto his aching erection. He thrust himself fully into her heat, his hands holding the firm globes of her buttocks.

She wrapped her legs around his hips. He found a nipple and sucked the hard bud into his mouth. He lifted her and thrust into her again. He lowered her back down his shaft and thrust again.

The contractions of her climax caressed him and went on and on, holding him in her hot, tight heat. Her arms clung to him for support. When her legs slipped from his hips, he carefully put one of his knees on the bed. Embedded deep in her, he lowered them both to the cool sheets. She looked at him, he bent and took her mouth, moving in her heat. He would make her come again before he satisfied himself. He caught her scream of pleasure in his mouth… and couldn't wait. He poured himself into her.

He *loved* her.

He loved what she did to his control. Her past no longer mattered. When they were satisfied, he pulled her into the curve of his body, kissed her damp brow and held her through the night.

CHAPTER 10

*L*iz awoke to the sun streaming in through the windows the next morning, and the bed empty. Rico's clothes were where he had dropped them the night before. She picked up his pants, folding them over her arm, then reached for his shirt. She froze. Her stomach knotted. On Rico's collar was a lipstick stain. It wasn't her lipstick.

Nausea rose into her throat. His clothes dropped from her hands. She left them where they fell and went into the bathroom to shower. Would she ever feel clean again? He had been with another woman and then come home to her. Oh, she hated him and what he was turning her into. She would confront him. She had to.

To take her away from everything she knew and then—on her first night in his home, leave her and be intimate with another woman? She tried not to think of what he'd done to her, how she'd begged, and how she loved every minute of his lovemaking. She was furious.

It was early morning still, so she peeked into Tony's room

to find him sleeping. She went down to the kitchen where Anna and Rosaria were talking.

"Good morning." Liz sat at the table.

"*Buon giorno, Signora DiMarco,*" Rosaria said as she brought Liz a cup of coffee.

"Thank you." Liz watched the steam slowly curl up from the black liquid, searching for answers.

"Look, we have a baby monitor," Anna said. "We can hear Tony when he wakes up."

Liz smirked. *Too bad I couldn't monitor where Rico went last night.* "That's great. With the size of this house, we would never find him." Just then, Tony's little voice came through the monitor.

"Mama, Mama."

Was he frightened? Liz flew out of the kitchen and up the stairs to his room. She ran into the nursery and came to a halt. Rico was on his haunches, holding Tony.

"Hello darling, were you scared?" Liz asked.

"Papa came."

Rico let go of Tony and stood. Tony ran to his mother for a hug.

"I'm sorry I wasn't here. I was in the kitchen with *Nonna.*" She pushed his hair out of his eyes. "Do you want to wash up? Then we can have breakfast together."

"Papa, the pony," Tony said, as he went to Rico.

Once more, Rico crouched down by his son. "After breakfast, we can go for a ride to see the pony I told you about."

Her eyes met Rico's black ones, questioning as her brows drew together. She mouthed, "A pony?"

"I want to go now." Tony stomped his feet.

"No. Remember, I told you the pony is sleeping. You have to do what Mama says."

Rico shrugged and said to Liz, "We will take a drive, and you will see."

After breakfast, Liz and Tony got into Rico's BMW for the ride into the mountains above Palermo.

~

RICARDO DROVE out of the city traffic and up winding roads with sharp curves, thinking back to last night. While making love to his wife, he'd realized just how much he loved her. It didn't matter that she had lied, or cheated, or kept his son from him.

He'd planned on spending an enjoyable evening with his mistress. Carolina was thirty-five, tall, blond, and beautiful. She'd lost her husband three years ago. Ricardo had been honest with her from the beginning, that he wouldn't commit to her, and that he had other women.

Last night, when he got to her home, he'd realized it was a mistake. Carolina kissed him and tried to hold him. He didn't feel any desire for her, not like he had in the past. Her embrace did nothing for him. The thought of kissing her no longer seemed inviting. Her lips weren't full and sensual like Liz's. He desired his wife and only his wife. Ricardo had removed himself from Carolina's clinging arms and told her he was now married and would no longer see her. She'd reached for him, but he held her back, saying he would deposit a substantial amount of money into her bank account. He would also sign the deed to the house she lived in over to her, so that she could live out her life in comfort.

Ricardo had wished her well, then went down the street to the corner bar and had a drink. He'd sat there for hours, thinking of his life and the deceitful gold digger that was now in his home, in his bed. He'd wondered if Andre had left Liz when he'd realized the baby she carried wasn't his. Who were those other men she'd slept with? There were more than a few that he was aware of—how could she have kept his son from him? Why hadn't she contacted him when she knew Tony was his son? Liz had named him as the father on the birth certificate.

He'd left the bar and gone home, planning to confront Liz and make her admit that she'd left him for Andre, and that she had left that man for yet another. Everything went a little crazy when he saw her sitting up in bed comfortably reading. Just like that, he wanted her. Above all, he'd needed to make sure she knew it was him, her husband. Always him. He'd almost told her he loved her.

He'd said the words in Italian, but she didn't know what, *ti amo* meant. He would have to be careful from now on.

Rico slowed the car as the road became a narrow gravel driveway. They had arrived at his ranch, up in the mountains, above Palermo.

Liz stepped out of the car, and Rico helped Tony out of his child seat. The BMW was parked by a stable, with a small stone cottage nearby. Tony wanted to run into the field where some horses were grazing.

Rico stopped him. "No. You must learn safety first. Then you can see the horses and the special pony that is yours."

Tony looked up at his father and took his hand. "Yes, Papa."

Liz smiled at Tony's docile reaction—she knew he would have stamped his feet and cried if she'd told him that he had to wait to see a pony. She relaxed—she'd always known that Rico would make a good father. Too bad he was so callous with her. *Why did he marry me? He wanted his son, that's why.* She huffed to herself, realizing that marrying her wouldn't stop him from seeing other women. Well, he couldn't have it both ways. He was the one who'd said he wanted a real marriage. She would show him what that meant.

Earlier that morning, she'd hidden his shirt with the lipstick stain in the closet. She wanted to keep the evidence to throw in his face when she told him she would no longer share a bed with him.

How could he? How could he have come from one woman's arms to her? Her mind burned with the memory, all those wonderful things he'd done with her last night. Telling her that he loved her in Italian. Oh, she understood that phrase well enough. But how could she trust him not to throw her out again? To have turned his back on her the way he did when he knew she was expecting his child.

She would keep her feelings to herself because of Tony, but she wouldn't make love with Rico while he went with other women. She had to keep some self-respect. She wouldn't allow him to treat her like the dirt under his feet, though he tried.

Tony's voice broke into her thoughts, "Mama, look at *my* pony! He's a nice pony." He patted it. "Papa said next time I can ride him!"

Liz looked at Rico in alarm. "Do not worry, *cara mia*. I will be with him."

He put his arm around her waist and whispered close to her ear, "I am having a custom saddle made for Antonio as well as a riding outfit. A Christmas present from both of us. Next time we come Antonio will ride with me on my horse."

Tony walked ahead of them, so Rico pulled Liz into his arms and brushed a kiss on her brow. "Remember in Bermuda when I rode my horse, and you rode me?"

Her cheeks flamed, and she turned her face away from him. He laughed and kissed her temple. "I will never forget that day we spent in Bermuda. You were shy then, but now you are a woman, who is not shy in her pleasure." He tilted his head toward Tony and said in a low, seductive voice, "When we have a private moment, I will show you."

Liz thought when they had a private moment, she would confront him with that shirt and tell him she wouldn't share his bed. She didn't want to be reminded of that day in Bermuda when she was young and in love with Rico. That beautiful day she had likely conceived Tony.

On the drive back to Palermo, Tony was excited about his pony. He had named him after one of his favorite superheroes. Rico brought them to a restaurant near a famous square where they had a nice lunch as a family. She and Rico laughed at how Tony enjoyed his spaghetti and meatballs. When lunch was finished, they got back into the car, and Tony promptly fell asleep on the short drive. Rico carried him up to his bedroom, and Liz put Tony down for a nap.

Liz read the note Anna had left, telling her that Massimo was taking her for a drive to her hometown, and she'd be gone for the rest of the day.

Rico's cell phone rang. His father needed to discuss a matter with him. Since Tony was sleeping, he went alone, leaving Liz on her own in the enormous house.

She wandered from room to room, realizing that the dining room where they had their meals wasn't the only one. There was another formal dining room with a huge table and high-back upholstered chairs. There was even a small ball-room—the wooden floor gleamed in the afternoon sunlight. The home was magnificent. Along the lines of a palace. There were marble floors throughout and a wide staircase that curved up to the second floor. There were six bedrooms, each suite with its own bathroom. An informal living room, with two sofas and comfortable armchairs. A smaller dining room with a round dining table.

The top floor was their private domain—the master bedroom with its walk-in-closets and dressing area. An attached bathroom with an enormous sunken tub in the center, against one wall stood a glass-enclosed shower. There was even a sitting room with a fireplace. Rico had his office and a home theater down the hall. She looked at the selection of DVDs, some in Italian that she couldn't read the titles of, but there in the mix were some in English.

She went into the sitting room and turned on the intercom so she could monitor the nursery, then reclined on the chaise lounge. The last couple of days had been tiring, with the time difference from New York to Sicily, and exhaustion finally caught up with her. Liz closed her eyes.

RICARDO FOUND HER ASLEEP. She looked beautiful, with her heart-shaped face and dark lashes fanning across her cheeks, flaming hair around her shoulders. His palms itched to comb through that luxurious mane of thick silk. Pink, full lips, almost too wide for her face, but just right. He wanted to run his tongue along her bottom lip before he sucked it into his mouth.

He had to turn away before he lifted the siren in his arms and carried her to bed. Instead, he covered her with a throw blanket, picked up the nursery monitor, and left her to sleep. He walked down the corridor with its curving wall of windows and went into his office to catch up on work, able to watch his son through the monitor.

Ricardo stared at his computer. Elbow propped on his desk, the palm of his hand on his chin, his fingers tapped his cheek.

Someone was trying to undermine one of his companies, buying stock, and attempting to position themselves for a takeover. He'd been aware of this for some time now. He and Gianni had made discreet inquiries—no sense alerting the stockholders. Massimo had been involved in the investigation as well.

His father had heard about the situation and wanted to know precisely how Ricardo planned on moving forward. During their meeting, Ricardo had assured him though, whoever was behind this covered their trail, Ricardo wouldn't let anyone outmaneuver him.

He heard Tony moving about, so he shut down his computer and went to get his son. Rosaria had milk and cookies ready for Tony. Ricardo sat with him and taught him to say thank you and milk and cookies, in Italian.

The little boy had so many questions. "How do I say pony?" They were laughing together when Liz came into the room, her hair mussed from sleeping. She straightened her skirt and blouse. Tony showed her his cookie. Liz ruffled his hair and kissed his cheek.

Ricardo looked deeply into her eyes, trying to read her thoughts. *Did she ever love me?* She turned and went to get herself a glass of water and sat with them. Tony scooted off to play with his toys.

Rico turned to Liz, "My parents wanted Antonio—"

"His name is Tony," she interrupted with some anger in her voice.

"Ah, *si*, but his birth certificate says Antonio."

"Yes, now that you changed it. You *had* no right."

"Oh, *cara mia*, but I am his father. I have every right."

She opened her mouth to say something more, but Rico cut her off and swished his hand through the air. "*Basta.* Enough. We will call him Tony, so he does not get confused."

She nodded.

"My parents would like *Tony*," he stressed the name, "to spend some time with them. Perhaps tomorrow we can bring him over for a few hours. My sister Julia is bringing her two little ones, Giovanni who is three and Daniella who is one.

The children will spend the night. Julia and her husband might be out late, and she does not like to leave them with a sitter."

Liz's brows furrowed, as if she weren't sure about letting Tony stay at his grandparents. Even though it would only be for the day. In the end, Rico convinced her that it would be good for Tony. It would help him adjust to his new life.

THAT EVENING, Rosaria prepared dinner for Rico, Liz, and Tony. After a quiet meal at home, Liz brought Tony upstairs for a bath and a bedtime story. Disturbed, she wondered how she would adjust to life here in Italy. *What would Rico do tonight? Would he go out to be with another woman?* She had to confront him about the lipstick stain. Today, there hadn't been a moment when they'd been alone. She took a deep breath as a wave of apprehension swept through her.

What she wanted to do involved throwing the shirt in his face. She wanted to rip it to shreds just as he had ripped her heart to shreds. She loved her son and would live this life so he could be with his father, but she wouldn't let Rico take her to bed and flaunt his women in her face.

She showered and got into bed, formulating a plan—she would pretend to be asleep should Rico want her. Tomorrow with Tony at his grandparents, she would be able to confront Rico. Her plan almost worked. She had gotten into bed, turned off the lights, and closed her eyes. She heard Rico come into the room as she lay there pretending to be asleep. She heard the shower turn on and relaxed, trying to fall asleep.

A little later, she felt the bed dip, and his strong arms came around her as he pulled her to his hard body.

"I know you are not asleep. Is this a new game you wish

to play? You know, *cara,* I always win." He held her to him, and she felt his erection against her buttocks. His hands moved to her breasts through her nightgown, and he plucked her nipples into hard peaks. His hot, open mouth seared her skin as he kissed along her neck and shoulder. She was furious at her vulnerability to him, she had to stop him, "Rico—"

"*Si, cara mia,* say my name. I love to hear my name on your luscious lips. When you moan, all I want to do is pleasure you more." His hand burned a path to her abdomen and then at the juncture of her legs. She groaned as her nightgown was bunched around her waist. His naked body at her back, he lifted her leg over his hip. His hand skimmed her abdomen, moving to her center. Anger and excitement jumbled in Liz. She felt herself weaken. He knew exactly what she liked.

His finger in her, arousing her, touched the sensitive nerves moving into her core.

"Please don't."

"Really?" His finger moved deeper into her. "I can feel how much you want me."

She huffed in exasperation, angry at her own body for betraying her. He kissed her neck, hot kisses... He touched her hip as he slowly pressed against her and slid in.

"You are so hot and tight." His knowing finger found the bud of her desire, pressing and circling. Her emotions melted her resolve, she didn't want to fight him anymore and wanted him deeper in her. She moved her buttocks back against him, and he slid into her.

"Ah *amore, si,* just like that." He kissed her neck, plucked her clitoris, and whispered, "Say my name."

She did. It came out half-moan, half-sigh. "Rico."

She felt the waves of her orgasm begin, and he thrust deeply several more times, bringing them both over the edge.

He breathed into her ear—she heard the whispered, *"Ti amo."* His arms tightened around her, and he held her through the night.

In the morning, Rico was gone. Liz lay there thinking of the night before and how easily she gave into him. He had called her *amore*, love, but how could she trust him not to hurt her again? She had to talk to him today. For her own sake and her son's.

Sicily's weather was mild in comparison to New York. She chose a red silk dress with nude-color high-heel shoes. She tied her hair up in a knot, knowing Rico didn't like it that way. This was her little way of keeping some of herself. She walked to Tony's room, but he wasn't there. She went down to the dining room, and there he was, all dressed and sitting next to Rico.

"Good morning, Mama." Tony slid out of his chair and came to her for a kiss. "Papa got me up and helped me dress." He had a broad smile on his chubby face, his black curls as unruly as ever and his black eyes so full of happiness. "I have cousins!" Liz helped him back into his booster seat. *Does he even know what cousins mean?*

Mid-morning, Rico and Liz brought Tony to his grand-parents' home. She met Rico's sister and her two children. Julia was very friendly and spoke perfect English. She invited Liz over to her home the following week.

Liz and Rico kissed Tony and left.

"Let us go for a drive," he said.

"Good. I need some fresh air." *And to be far away from your bed when we talk.*

RICARDO KEPT his eyes on the road as he pointed out the vineyard separating his property from his cousin Giorgio's.

He gestured toward the lemon and orange groves. He showed her the almond trees and pointed to the olive grove in the distance. It produced olive oil for DiMarco Enterprises. Liz seemed to relax, not sitting so stiff.

"It's so beautiful." She glanced at him. "I can see the Mediterranean in the distance."

He parked in front of the villa. "Come, let us go in so you can see the house." He took her hand, intertwining their fingers, and led her to the front door.

Rico opened the door.

"Oh…" Liz murmured.

He bent his head, gazing at her.

"Oh, it's beautiful… so light… and all these windows."

"Let me show you the rest of the house. There are five bedrooms, a library, and a study."

Liz turned to Rico, smiling. "This house is beautiful." She shrugged and tilted her head to the side. "I keep saying that, but it is. You said it's yours, but who lives here?"

He looked into her green eyes. "You can if you wish."

Liz blinked, her head jerked, and she took a step back as if he had slapped her.

Dɪᴅ Rico want her out of his life? She knew he didn't love her. The words he whispered while making love meant nothing to him. He was done with her and again throwing her out. Maybe this time he would keep her in this nice house for her son's sake. *I will live here while he stayed where? Palermo?*

"I—" She swallowed past the lump that grew in her throat. "I don't… understand. You want me… to live here?"

"If you like. It will be better for Tony."

Her lips thinned in anger. Her nostrils flared, and one

auburn brow lifted. "And you? Oh… I see. Then you can stay in your grand palazzo and bring your women there. So easy and convenient with me hidden away here."

He raised his head, looking down his nose. A mocking smile edged across his face. "What are you talking about? You are the cheat with your deceit and lies. The one who cannot be satisfied by one man." His accent got thicker with each word. He ran his fingers through his jet-black hair.

Liz looked away for a moment. He would never believe her, never believe that he was the only man she had ever been with.

When she turned back, his mocking smile was gone, and she saw the fury on his face as his black eyes spat fire at her. He whirled and stormed to the car. Rico jerked open the passenger door, and with anger and disgust in his voice, said, "Get in. Let us go."

She raised her nose in the air, walking past him with stiff dignity and slid into the car. He slammed the door with such force, the BMW shook. He stalked around the front of the car, his lips thin, his jawbone clenched. He was in a towering rage. She'd never seen him so angry. The old Rico, the one she'd fallen in love with, had always been so calm, loving.

With jerking motions, he yanked his door open and got into the driver's seat. The car shook a second time as he slammed his own door. He turned on the ignition and revved the engine, threw it into gear, and sped off toward the city. Her own anger skyrocketed. She'd confront him as soon as they got home. They rode in silence.

The drive home had done nothing to calm their anger. Rico stopped the car in front of the palazzo. Liz threw open the car door and stalked up the stone walkway to the front door. Rico walked around her and opened the heavy wood and leaded-glass entry door.

Liz ran past him, through the entry, and up the main

staircase to the master suite. She hurried into the walk-in-closet and grabbed his shirt from where she hid it. She turned and almost bumped into him. "Here." She shook the rumpled shirt under his nose. "Look at this. The night you came home and made love with me—you liar—you had this shirt on." She showed him the exact stain. "See the lipstick on the collar? That is *not* mine. You came from another's arms. How could you?" She threw the shirt at his face and ran from the room.

Rico grabbed her, spun her to face him, and held her upper arms. Liz turned her head away from him.

"You have the nerve to accuse me of sleeping around?" Rico dropped his hands from her and paced away, then turned back with a look of disgust on his handsome face. His inky-black eyes ran up and down her body. "Why you lying cheat, you left me to go with all those other men." His voice vibrated through her. "You are going to pay and pay dearly for this."

He lunged at her, then a look of horror came over his face. He stood still. In a voice that held no emotion, just a command of certainty, he said, "Get out. I want you to pack your bags and get out of my home. And by the way, my dear, dishonest, lying wife, *I am* going to keep my son with me."

CHAPTER 11

"I won't go without my son," Liz shouted. Deep down, she knew that Ricardo would never raise his hands to a woman. He'd come close to slapping her just now though he'd caught himself.

"It is too bad." A sneer crept across his sensual lips as he said with contempt, "My son has to have a mother like you."

Liz reached for the bedpost. Had Rico slapped her, it would have been less painful than that tone. She supported herself so she wouldn't crumble to the floor. Her chest constricted, hot tears stung her eyes, and a lump formed in her throat.

Ricardo strode out of the bedroom.

Liz closed her eyes, searching for calm. She had to compose herself before she could try to talk to him. *What was he... talking about? Other men. What other men?* Thinking of all the terrible things he had said, her anger soared. Her cheeks felt hot. She stormed down the hall and found him in his office. He sat at his desk, in a high-back leather chair, staring at a blank computer screen.

She cleared her throat. Ricardo didn't acknowledge her.

She slammed her hands on the front of his desk, arms spread, palms flat, and leaned over from the waist.

He turned.

She almost jumped away. His face was a mask of rage. Her own anger kept her from fleeing.

"How many times must I tell you, you, big oaf? You are the only one I have ever been with. You. Only you." She lifted one hand from his desk and stabbed the air before him with her pointing finger. "You threw me out. You didn't even have the *decency* to tell me yourself."

Her anger grew as he ignored her. While she yelled, Ricardo sat in his leather chair, looking so calm. He rested one elbow on the arm of his chair, his chin on his hand.

The heat of her fury raced through her body. How could she reach him?

Rico opened the top drawer of his desk and removed a large envelope. He placed it in the center. With both hands, he slowly slid the envelope toward Liz.

"Here," he said harshly. "You cannot deny these."

Liz picked up the heavy envelope, opened the flap, and pulled out a stack of photos. She looked at a picture and gasped. "Oh my." She saw herself in bed with another man. As she flipped through the pile of photos, her eyes rounded, and her mouth dropped open in disbelief.

"How could this be?" she whispered as she stared at another photo, physically ill. The images were purely pornographic. Liz sank into the brown leather chair facing Rico's desk. The woman in the photos certainly looked like her, but how could it be? She never—

"No. Andre! But how?" She'd met him once when Rico had taken her on a cruise to celebrate their six-month anniversary. She'd barely said two words to the man.

"Rico, these have to be photoshopped." She glanced up

from the photos just in time to see a smirk on his sculpted lips.

He shook his head. "No, they are not. I own the negatives."

"Impossible."

With a smug expression, he said, "What more lies will you tell me, *cara*, to get out of this? You are now holding the proof of *your* deceit."

She wanted to wipe that arrogant expression off his face. There had to be an explanation. She wasn't crazy. Wouldn't she remember who she slept with? Especially since it had only ever been Rico.

Liz grabbed the pile of photos again and flipped through them. She was on her back, legs spread, and Andre on top of her naked body. She stopped and scrutinized another photo. No doubt the woman resembled her. There had to be a way that her face was superimposed onto someone else. It *had* to be. "These photos aren't me. It's a trick, I would know…" Her voice trailed off.

"When I first received them, I had the same thought. That someone had played a terrible trick on us. I was contacted anonymously and for an astronomical amount of money, I could buy the negatives."

Liz sat on the edge of the leather chair, holding the pictures, studying them. There were some of her in bed with men other than Andre. She made two piles of photos on his desk. Peering closely at the one she held in her hand, she frowned. It was of the woman on top, straddling the man. She found a close-up of the same pose which showed the woman's backside. Liz used her fingernail to scrape at what appeared to be dirt, but it wouldn't come off. She searched for another photo of the woman's backside. She found one, and her hand trembled as she stared. The same mark. She picked up another, and there it was again. She looked into Rico's cold eyes. His mocking smile.

"See this." Liz pointed to the mark. "This woman has a birthmark on her buttock. The same marking is in *all* the photos of her backside."

Rico moved forward in his chair. "Where? Let me see." He reached for the pictures. Rico examined each one of them. Then he took the negatives out of their protective sleeves and examined them with a magnifying glass. "You are correct. The person in the photo has a birthmark. I know your body is not marred by any markings… I was rash and only glanced at the photos." He smiled. "You do have a beauty mark on the underside of your right breast. I love to run my tongue along it."

"This *is serious*. Who did this?"

"I do not know, but I will find out."

The only sound was the tick-tock of an antique clock that hung on the wall. The silence dragged on. She lifted her gaze, and time seemed to stop.

He slid his chair back. "We have much to sort out." He stood, came around his desk, and knelt by Liz. "*Amore mio. My love.* Can you ever forgive me for being so blind? Now I can see that the woman in the photos does not have your beautiful body."

His mouth curved into a smile. "Why do you not remove that dress?" He wiggled his brows at her. "So, I can be absolutely certain you do not have a mark on your lovely bottom." His arms went around her waist.

"No!" She grabbed at his hands, trying to remove them from her waist. "First you accuse me of all sorts of vile things, then you tell me to pack my bags, threaten to take my son, and now you want me to undress for you?" Her voice rose with her indignation. "I can't believe how insensitive—"

"The photos were quite damaging." His arms tightened around her waist.

Her voice, when she spoke, held a mix of fear and anger—fear that her body would insist what her brain was denying. "No, Rico. Stop."

He rose to his feet and gently pulled her to stand. He walked over to the leather couch, sat, and tugged her on his lap. Liz kept her back stiff and straight, refusing to relax against him. She slid off his lap and moved to the far end of the couch.

He cleared his throat. "You accused me of going to another woman, having sex with her, and then coming home to make love with you… Well, I will tell you… it is partly true."

Liz arched her brow and looked into his black-as-night eyes.

He continued, "I wasn't celibate after you left me—I had mistresses, *cara*, but not one of them could compare to what we had shared. When my father had a heart attack, I moved back to Sicily. I met Carolina. She and I attended high school together. She had been recently widowed when I returned home. We had an understanding. She would be mine exclusively, and I would take care of her. That night, when we first arrived, I went to her home."

Liz's back straightened, her nostrils flaring. She bit her bottom lip.

"You may accuse me of the intention, *amore*, but not the deed. I told Carolina that I was now married. She didn't care, but *I* did. There is only one woman I have ever wanted, and that… is *you*." He reached for her hand. Liz moved farther away. "I left her apartment and went to have a drink at the bar, then I came home to you." She shook her head. "There is one other thing I want to say to you."

Liz shifted her eyes to glance at him.

"Earlier when I asked you if you wanted to live in the villa, I never meant without me. I want us to live there together." His hand slid across the space separating them. "I bought that house soon after we had met, always with the intention of one day you and I living there, making babies, and raising our family together. It has always been you. Please, Liz, can you ever forgive me for my brutish behavior?"

Liz rushed back into his arms and sat on his lap.

"*Amore*, we will work all this out and move forward."

Her arms twined around his neck. "Oh, Rico, so much has gone wrong. How did you get those terrible pictures? Is that why you sent me away?"

Ricardo didn't want to talk right now—all he wanted was to cover her warm, inviting mouth with his. The kiss started out gentle, but he had four years of wanting her to make up for. He crushed her curves to him, but that wasn't enough. He wanted her naked.

His fingers were gentle on her chin, going to her collarbone around to her back, seeking the zipper. The dress parted down her spine. Liz took her arms out of the dress and wiggled so that it laid around her waist. Rico unclasped the delicate lacy bra to reveal her perfect, full breasts. He took a nipple into his mouth, flicking it with his tongue, tantalized it until the nipple became a hard bud. He treated the other with the same exquisite care.

Liz quivered on his lap, the curve of her hip against his already hard shaft. His hand moved up her leg until he met the satin-smooth bare skin above her thigh-high nylons. Higher, to the juncture of her shapely legs, touching the lace of her panties, cupping her woman's mound.

Rico kissed the corner of her mouth and nibbled on her lower lip, devouring its softness. She lifted her hands into his hair. Holding his head, she pressed her lips more firmly to his, pulling him closer. He stood her before him and shimmied the dress down her body. Her face was already flushed with desire as she stepped out of the cascading fabric. He slid the stockings down her shapely legs and threw them to the side, onto the pile of clothing.

He gazed into her smoldering emerald-green eyes.

"Take the panties off." Rico's deep, husky voice made her shiver.

Liz hooked her thumbs into the elastic and slid the lace down her legs. "Will you take *your* clothes off?"

"Not yet." The smile he gave her sent her pulse racing.

"Come here." Rico took her hips in his big hands, moving her forward to straddle him. Her naked body against the roughness of his slacks added to her desire. His head dipped, and he took her breast, his tongue moving on the erect nipple. She massaged his nape, running her fingers through his thick hair, pulling him closer to her breast.

His hands at her hips, she felt his bulging erection at her abdomen and sat back on his lap. Her fingers trembled as she unfastened first one, then another and another of his shirt buttons. She needed to feel him in her body. She tried to unzip his pants, but he brushed her hands away. Rico reached between their bodies, his hand on her abdomen, spreading heat as he traced a path into her tight red curls, and found the bud of her desire, circling the flesh. His finger dipped into her.

Once more, she skimmed her fingers down to his waist, needing to unfasten his pants.

"No, *amore*." He moved her hands to her sides. "First you, maybe more than once," he kissed her neck, "then me."

She groaned, her body moving forward. With his arms around her waist, Rico stood, held her hand, and walked over to his desk. With one broad, swift motion, he swiped the photos onto the floor. His lips found hers, and she reached up on tiptoe to fit herself against his hard body. He lifted her onto the edge of his desk. "Lie down for me." His lips trailed kisses down the curve of her neck.

He gently eased her down, taking one hard nipple into his mouth. His hand moving on her stomach, he kissed a path of fire to her abdomen. His hands moved to her legs, spreading them.

He was going to make her crazy, she was sure of that. His large hands slid from her knees to her inner thighs. When his thumbs moved to spread her red curls, he touched the tip of his tongue to her center. Her breath hitched, but he wouldn't do more. She lifted her abdomen, trying to get closer. She reached for his head, her fingers going into his hair, massaging his scalp. "Rico—"

He did all the things Liz loved, pressing his tongue to her bud of nerves then circling as she called his name. He pulled her closer to the edge of the desk, moving her feet to his shoulders, opening her to his lips and tongue. She was going crazy, and she knew he hadn't even begun to torture her.

She felt him spread her wider, his thumbs massaging her flesh. Licking her, then he thrust his tongue deep into her center. Her buttocks shot off the desk, his wicked, knowing tongue doing all the things he taught her to need to love. She felt the waves of ecstasy pulsing through her. Her fingers, in his hair relaxed, as her legs followed.

When the contractions of her climax stopped, he moved a finger into her passage and sucked on her throbbing bud. She cried out at the pleasure. Her fingers moved back into his hair. When he added a second finger, her back arched off the desk, the pleasure so great. She moaned as her hips moved in wild abandon. He put his forearm across her abdomen to hold her in place.

Sucking, licking, then the tip of his tongue pressed on her clit, as his fingers thrust into her heat, searching for her G-spot. She held his head closer. Her legs had slipped over his broad shoulders, and the heels of her feet dug into his back. Her body arched as his finger found the spot. She took one hand out of his hair to cover her mouth and tried not to scream… She did scream when the waves of that second orgasm washed over her.

RICO STAYED with her until the last ripple of pleasure ended. Her legs were limp, her body flat on the desk, and her cheeks flushed. He stood, unzipped his pants, and stepped out of them. He lifted her into his arms and walked to the nearest empty wall. There was no way he could wait to go to the bedroom.

Her arms came around his neck, he held her waist, leaned the curve of her back on the wall, and lifted her higher, her legs went around him. With one sure thrust, he impaled her onto his aching need. Her head rolled from side to side, silky auburn hair flowing around her, the flush of pleasure on her face, neck and breasts. She called his name, "Rico."

He loved the feel of her tight, honeyed heat. She was hotter than Etna when it erupted. He buried himself deeper into Liz. The sound of his name on her kiss-swollen lips drove him on. Her legs around his hips, her ankles locked behind him, the satin-smooth globes of her buttocks in his hands. Rico drove her to another climax. Her hands gripped his shoulders, the taut nipples of her breasts rubbed against his chest.

"Come with me," she said in a tremulous whisper.

His lips brushed against hers as he spoke, "The next one, *amore mio. Ti amo.*"

She moved forward, kissing his shoulders, his neck. He couldn't get enough of her. He thrust again and again. When she climaxed, he let go of his control. Two shuddering thrusts into her heat, allowing her passage to stroke him, surround him. She almost slid down the wall, but he caught her behind the knees. Liz lifted her arms to gently loop around his neck. Her eyes closed, a contented smile spread on her flushed face. Her head rested on his shoulder, and her hand went to the nape of his neck, curling his hair around her finger.

He carried her down the hall, with its wall of glass windows, to their bedroom. Rico laid her on the bed, sat next to her, and pulled the covers up over them. He nipped her bottom lip. "A good argument is sometimes needed to clear the air."

She fell asleep in his arms, a smile on her lips.

ONLY SEVEN DAYS had gone by since Rico had come back into her life. So much had happened in that short time. Now Liz couldn't blame him for thinking the worst of her. Those photographs had been pretty convincing. She had almost doubted herself, that somehow, she had been drugged. At least now he knew the truth. She had never cheated on him.

She thought back to all those empty years without Rico. From time to time, she had gotten a glimpse of him on the cover of some flashy magazine. Always a stunning, tall blonde on his arm, though never the same one. Liz would have loved to read the story, but she couldn't afford the price of the magazine. *Rico had always protected her from the media.* He'd worked hard to keep their relationship out of the press. As one of the richest men in the world, with his good looks and charisma, it hadn't been easy.

Once at the supermarket, Tony asleep in her arms, she'd seen Rico's tall figure, dressed in a tuxedo, on the cover of a magazine by the checkout. Billionaire Mogul to Marry Model-Girlfriend. She'd stared at the cover. Was this who he'd left her for? Devastated, she'd hugged Tony, the son he hadn't wanted, closer to her. She paid for the milk and bread and left the store, tears stinging the backs of her eyes. By the time she reached home, they'd spilled down her cheeks.

Anna saw the tears and had settled Tony down in his bassinet. She sat on the couch next to Liz, and between sobs, Liz told Anna all about Rico—all except that he had given her money to have an abortion. That part she couldn't even acknowledge.

From that day, she and Anna had an unspoken agreement never to mention Rico. Liz knew there were many nights Anna had heard her crying, but in the morning, Anna never mentioned anything. Liz learned how to move on. The first time she'd had to leave Tony to go to work was the worst day of her life. The only thing that kept her going was the knowledge that at least her precious baby was with Anna. Eventually, she'd found a better job with steady hours.

Liz sighed and brought herself back to the present. When she'd gotten the job at the jewelry store, the pay had been so much more substantial, they'd struggled a little less, and she was almost out of debt.

RICO SUGGESTED that since Tony wanted to spend the night with his grandparents and cousins, he and Liz could go out to dinner. She had taken her time choosing from the new dresses that hung in her closet. She picked out a burgundy, off the shoulder cocktail dress. It hugged her in all the right places. Nude nylons and silver high heels finished the outfit. Liz carried a small beaded clutch.

She patted her dress, smoothed her hair, and walked out of the dressing room to meet him.

Rico stood from the sofa, dressed in one of his many custom-made suits, when she entered the sitting room, "Ah, *bella.* You are beautiful." He kissed her hand, then picked up a high-gloss, cream-colored wooden box from the side table. The center of the lid was inlaid with two interlinking hearts, and a yellow rose in each heart. Liz recognized the jewelry box. Rico had it especially made for her in Sorrento and shipped to New York.

"I have kept these safe for you," he said as he held the custom-made wooden box out to her.

She peered into his pitch-black, fathomless eyes, her mouth rounding in an O. She glanced at the box in his hands. She knew what it held. All the gifts of jewelry he had given her. His smile was brilliant.

"Rico, I—"

"They are yours. Choose something to wear for tonight."

Her hands trembled as she took the jewelry box from him. She walked into the dressing room and gently placed the box on her dressing table, amazed that he had kept the jewels. He hadn't sold them or given them to his new girl-friends. She raised the lid, and memories flooded her. Tucked in the blue velvet-lined interior rested the diamond heart pendant he had bought her for their six-month anniversary.

The yellow diamond pendant he'd brought home just because it was her favorite color. The diamond earrings and bracelet he'd given her for her birthday. Memories of that night filled her. Her fingers touched the strand of pearls. Rico had gifted her those while they were in Bermuda.

Liz saw the ruby and diamond choker with the matching bracelet and drop earrings and chose that set to wear. It was one of the last gifts he had given her. She held the choker to her neck and glanced at him through the dressing table mirror. "Help me fasten this please."

He secured the clasp and dropped kisses down the back of her neck. His strong arms slipped around her waist, pulling her against his hard body. She tipped her head to one side. His warm lips kissed a path to her bare shoulder.

He breathed near her ear, "*Amore,* if we do not go now, we will not get to the restaurant tonight."

Liz smiled at his words and turned in his arms. "Though that is a very tempting invitation, we really didn't eat today, and I'm starving."

"Well, then, let us go. Far be it from me to deny you nourishment. You are too thin as it is." Rico held her hand as they went down the stairs to his waiting car. "I have come to realize that you neglected yourself to feed our son."

CHAPTER 12

Ricardo held the door of his Lamborghini open for Liz. He couldn't get enough of her sweet body, but they did have to eat. He drove to his favorite restaurant on the rooftop of an old palazzo that had been turned into a hotel. The food, homecooked, and the atmosphere romantic on the terrace where diners were seated at private tables covered in fine linen. Crystal glasses caught the light from the candles, making a prism of blue and violet dots on the white tablecloths.

As the sun set over the Mediterranean, the yellow glow turned the terracotta roof tiles bronze. The dome of the ancient cathedral across the way reflected the changing light from soft yellow to gold. Once the night arrived, it was difficult to make out the mountains in the distance.

Rico held the stem of his wine glass in his long fingers. "My family is back from their shopping spree in New York. Tomorrow, my parents are going to host a welcome home dinner and a formal dance. At that time, I will announce that we are married and have a son." He sipped his wine.

Her head came up, red-gold curls bounced in the candle glow, and her emerald eyes searched his. He couldn't miss the frown on her heart-shaped face. She put her fork down, the creamy risotto untouched.

He reached for her hand. "Do not fret so. It is only close family and some friends. They will be happy for us, just as my parents, sister, and brother-in-law are." A chuckle rumbled deep in his chest. "My mother wanted to have a big party with wedding cake and champagne." He saw her eyes round in fear. "Do not worry, she will not do anything to upset you."

"I know, it's just so much, Rico, with Gianni and Sofia's wedding coming up. I hope you understand… I would rather keep a low profile."

"Everything will be well. I realize you and Tony have much to adjust to." His fingers slid up her satin-smooth arm. "Eat. *amore mio,* the risotto here is the best in Sicily."

She gave him a smile as she reached for her fork.

He leaned forward, his voice soft, "Tomorrow, I will have to meet with my father, Massimo, and Gianni. I will be at the office most of the day."

She looked at him. "I understand. Tony will keep Anna and me busy."

He didn't want to tell Liz what he suspected. He knew someone was trying to take over the Contessa Cruise Line of DiMarco Enterprises. Buying blocks of stock. After the first of the year, there would be a board of directors meeting and a shareholders meeting scheduled in New York. Ricardo was determined to expose the person before the meetings. He knew, without a doubt, that the guilty party would try to make a grab for the company at the shareholders meeting. Ricardo would never let that happen. He didn't want Liz to worry, but he would find the real woman in the photos. He wanted to know who'd paid her and how Andre was involved.

After dinner, Rico and Liz strolled through a piazza near the restaurant, one of many squares in Palermo, decorated for Christmas. The large live tree that stood next to the cathedral was decorated with the top third in green lights, the middle section in white, and the bottom in red. Christmas colors as well as the colors of the Italian flag. Clear white lights with a star in the middle were strung across the street. There was a festive feel in the air as people walked about. Liz and Ricardo held hands and listened to the Christmas music.

Liz glanced at him. "The words are in Italian, but the tune sounds like Jingle Bells."

He laughed and hugged her to him. "Yes, that's exactly it." Then he kissed the tip of her nose. They continued walking around the piazza, and she sang the words in English.

THE FOLLOWING evening a limousine waited out front of the palazzo, ready to transport them to the gala event. Liz chose an emerald-green strapless gown the exact color of her eyes. She wore her engagement ring and wedding band along with diamond earrings and a necklace. Rico looked dashing in his tuxedo, and Tony was a miniature of his father. Anna wore a black gown, her hair pinned up in a French twist, and the diamond earrings Rico had given her as a thank you gift dangled on her ears. Massimo arrived, and they all left for the festivities.

The party was in full swing by the time the small group reached his parents' villa. Waiters carrying round silver trays served drinks in crystal flutes and hors d'oeuvres on china plates. Family and friends mingled and laughed. They talked about the fun they'd had in New York City, going to

Broadway shows, shopping along Fifth Avenue. The blizzard that stranded them. After an hour, Liz and Julia brought the children upstairs and put them to bed.

When Liz came back down the stairs to rejoin the party, she walked over to Ricardo who'd been talking to his father Giuseppe. "Liz, I hope you are enjoying yourself and not overwhelmed by all of this." He stretched his arm to encompass the room. Ricardo put his arm around her waist, giving her a gentle squeeze while she replied to her father-in-law.

"You have all been so welcoming to Tony and me. I feel extremely comfortable, thank you."

"We are waiting for my sister Angela Lombardo and my nephew Giorgio before I make the announcement of your marriage. They should be here soon."

As Giuseppe finished speaking, Rico's Aunt Angela arrived. A petite woman who Liz remembered always wore mourning black although her husband had been dead for more than twenty years. Her pitch-black hair was in a bun on top of her head, the only jewelry she wore was a string of pearls around her neck. Angela had gone directly over to Giuseppe, kissing him on both cheeks.

Rico greeted the man who'd accompanied Angela. "Hi Giorgio, come here. I want you to meet Liz, my wife." Giorgio was just as tall and handsome as the other DiMarco men, although his eye color was aqua blue. While he extended his hand to Liz, she saw Angela's head snap around to gape at her. "Nice to meet you, Giorgio." Liz was grateful that Rico had his arm around her waist.

She heard Giuseppe say to Angela, "Ah, you see Ricardo's wife. It was a big surprise to us."

"I thought I recognized you, Liz." Angela walked across the small space and came over to Liz. "I am so very glad to see you after all these years." Angela kissed her on both cheeks and gave her a big hug. "What a pleasant surprise."

Angela's voice dripped honey, "We will have to get together soon, go to lunch. You must tell me what you have been doing."

Liz, unable to respond, just nodded. Angela excused herself and strolled into the crowd, laughing, and greeting other guests.

"Welcome to the family, Liz." He kissed her on the cheek, and then he said loud enough for Rico to hear, "How did my cousin get so lucky to marry a beauty like you?" Then he left to talk to some of the other guests.

Rico held Liz's, hand and cocked his head, he whispered, "You are ice cold. Is all well with you?"

"Yes, I'm fine."

He hesitated.

Liz nodded. "Really… everything is fine."

"Good, my father, as head of the DiMarco family, is going to make the announcement. Be prepared for lots of hugs and kisses; they are a typical Italian family."

She gave him what she hoped was a glowing smile. He kissed her on the temple and put his arm around her waist. The announcement was made, and champagne served. Ricardo's family gathered to congratulate them with cheers and shouts of "*Auguri.*" Best wishes.

Rico and Liz smiled, then someone yelled, "Kiss her."

Liz's cheeks flushed. Ricardo bent and brushed her lips with his. The guests cheered and toasted the couple. Liz and Rico mingled, then Julia came over. "I'm going to check on the children."

"Oh, good—wait for me." Liz turned to Rico. "I'm going with Julia. I won't be long."

He kissed her brow.

When Liz came down the stairs after checking on Tony and his cousins, she walked out onto the balcony to clear her mind. The party had become stifling. Angela followed her.

"Oh, Liz, it is good that you and Ricardo are together. I understand that you have kept your baby." She leaned closer to whisper, "I tell him you would not give up your baby. You would never have an abortion." She sighed and continued, "But hot-blooded young men—what do they really know? They only have sex, they may say it is love, but we women know better."

Angela held Liz's left hand, admiring the five-carat diamond engagement ring and wedding band. "I hope for your sake he can give up his other women and be faithful to you."

Liz stiffened, unable to hide her distress.

In the past few days, Liz had put those thoughts out of her mind. Now, Angela had Liz wondering the same thing. Could she really trust Rico not to hurt her further? Angela was the only one who knew how badly Rico had betrayed her trust. Not wanting her or her baby. Anna didn't even know the full extent of what Rico had written in that note. All the bad memories came flooding back to twist her heart.

"There you are." Ricardo walked out to the balcony. "There you are Liz. Ciao, zia." He greeted his aunt and then took Liz back into the ballroom.

Hours later, the limousine stopped in front of the palazzo. Liz went ahead to open the front door. Rico carried their sleeping son up the stairs to his bedroom. Tony was already in his pajamas, so Rico laid him down, pulled the covers up, and kissed him on his forehead. He whispered, "Sweet dreams."

The way he cared for his son touched Liz's heart. Melting a little more of the ice that surrounded it. Angela's words came back to haunt her. She tried not to let Angela destroy the trust that once again grew between her and Ricardo.

In his own way, she knew Rico was considerate of her

feelings. Willing to marry her even when he thought the worst—that she had slept with all those men.

Those photos had almost convinced her. That woman in the pictures, who was she? Whoever did that had searched for the perfect double. Why? Who would want to hurt Rico and her so much? She and Rico hadn't discussed any of that, but they needed to.

They walked out of Tony's room together. Rico lifted Liz's hand and placed a kiss in the center of her palm as his black eyes held hers. "Thank you for a beautiful son, and for raising him so well while we were apart."

She leaned into him, grateful that he realized how hard she'd worked to nurture Tony. He wrapped his strong arms around her and bent to kiss her. His cologne mixed with his scent filled her as his lips softly brushed hers. His hands roamed over her bottom, pulling her closer to his strong, hard body. She loved the feel of him, his broad shoulders, his biceps, the muscles moving under her fingers. She had missed him so much, and his hands felt too good. Liquid heat spread into her center. Standing on the landing outside their son's room, she wanted Rico.

He lifted her into his arms. "It will be better if we go to our room," he whispered close to her ear, sending a thrill up her spine.

"Why?"

"There I can strip you naked and pleasure you to my heart's content over and over until you cry out my name." The tip of his tongue caressed the half circle of her ear. His lips moved down the side of her neck. She thought it was a good thing he carried her, or she would have melted in a puddle at his feet.

When he reached their room, he shouldered the ornate white and gold carved door leading to their suite and walked to the dressing room. He placed her in front of the oval standing mirror that resided on her side of the room. He stood behind her and unfastened the diamond necklace. She removed her earrings first one, then the other. Rico extended his palm upward, and she dropped the earring in his large hand. He put the jewelry on top of her dressing table.

He searched out the zipper at the side of her gown; her eyes met his black ones in the mirror. He held her against him. The smile he gave her had her pulses racing as he bent and kissed the side of her neck. Her breasts felt tight in the bodice, her nipples taut. He slowly unzipped the strapless gown. She lifted one arm to capture his head, her fingers tangling in his thick black hair. Her eyes closed in the pleasure of the moment as the gown pooled at her feet.

She looked at her reflection in the mirror and his eyes on her body, her naked breasts— the nipples peeking through her cascading hair were extended, begging for his touch. Her stockings were held up by the lacy garter around her waist. The elastic of the sheer panties hugged her hips, the front making a V, like an arrow pointing the way to her core. His hand slid over the skin of her belly and into the V, finding her center.

As his finger slid along the crease, she mewled.

"Spread your legs, *amore.*" The hot breath of his whisper at her ear drew a moan from her. "Look in the mirror."

She leaned back against him, her bottom rested between his legs. She braced her hands, her fingers spread on the hard muscles of his thighs. His touch on her breast was fire, and his lips trailed a similar blaze along her neck. She sunk farther onto his questing finger, hidden from her view, only feeling the slide from her center to touch her clit, before plunging back into her vagina.

She stared at herself. Rico's eyes held hers while he thrust his finger into her, kissing her neck, and she moved against his hard body. Her buttocks rubbed against him. He plucked at a taut nipple. She burned. Her legs opened wider. She grabbed at his thighs, her fingers clenching and unclenching. She threw her head back against his massive chest, unable to stop the sounds she made as his finger teased her and moved to trace her clit before he thrust into her again. He rained kisses down the side of her neck. Her hips rolled as her pelvis tightened.

Her lids closed in bliss.

"Keep your eyes on us in the mirror, *amore mio*," he whispered and licked her neck.

She breathed in his spicy cologne, and her head rolled on his shoulder. His fingers stopped the delicious torture.

"Oh." Her head came forward off his shoulder. "Rico, please, please, don't stop." She panted, undulating her hips.

"Look in the mirror—feel what I am doing to your body."

Her lids felt like lead as she opened her eyes. "Yes, I, I, oh, oh… y e s."

His finger moved in her again. He plucked at her nipple, while he thrust into her core. Sinking back onto his thighs, her buttocks pressed against his, oh-so-hard erection. His finger buried in her as the coil in her belly wound tighter with each thrust, his lips on her neck, sending shivers of heat throughout her body. His gaze caught hers in the mirror, just as the coil unwound into the waves of her climax.

"Rico," she called his name. He kept her at that high pitch of pleasure until her knees buckled. He picked her up and carried her out of the dressing room to their bed. He had stripped her of her panties and garter before laying her in the bed.

She watched him as he pulled his clothes off, flinging them to the floor, while she removed her shoes and rolled down her thigh-high nylons.

Rico sat on the bed. His broad shoulders propped against the headboard. He wiggled his brows at Liz.

She wasn't sure what he wanted, but then she smiled and lifted herself up to straddle his middle. Bit by bit, oh so slow, she took his huge steel hard erection into her. "You feel so good." She came forward, offering her breasts.

Rico held her hips, buried deep in her, and sucked a taut nipple into his mouth. Laving it, before moving on to the other one.

She moved on him just the way he'd taught her to. He held her on his hard length. She set the pace, bringing her closer and closer to another climax. Her contractions held him, moving to take all his length into her body, sending him over the edge to join her. She fell on his chest, the thud of his heartbeat under her cheek. She lay wrapped around him. His hands massaged her back and buttocks, and Liz fell asleep in his arms.

During the night, she had rolled to her side. He'd covered them both and, in the morning when she woke, he still held her. She looked at his handsome face, thinking back to last night. She would never see her reflection in a mirror without remembering what he had done to her. The desire on her face… how her eyes smoldered when he made her climax. Watching herself and feeling her muscles clenching around his finger. That was what he saw when he looked at her orgasm. It was an unexpected gift from him.

She knew how he looked, with his chiseled features, intent on bringing them both the greatest pleasure she'd ever felt. She remembered her panic when he'd stopped because she had closed her eyes. She had no idea how much she'd missed this man until now. Her heart melted even more. She thought that if he touched her, she would go to him again. Her eyes shifted to the sheet covering them and gasped. His side was tented over his middle.

Liz heard his sexy, deep laugh and then his voice, "Don't look so surprised. The way you were looking at me made me want you all over again. I know it may be too late. We should have discussed this sooner, but I have to say I want at least four maybe five sons before we have a daughter. How do you feel about that?"

She looked at him and ran her fingers through his dark chest hairs, her leg resting on his thigh.

"Well, I was an only child and didn't like it one bit. I… think it may be… too late to ask me though. I'm not on any form of birth control and you…" Liz looked away. "Well, you haven't—I mean… with the amount of lovemaking—what I'm trying to say… is I may very well *be* pregnant."

She thought back to the time in Bermuda when he had coaxed her onto his horse. He'd held her in front of him, his big hands under her yellow sundress played with her breasts. Then he turned her in his strong arms to straddle him. The motion of the horse… his condom broke, and that was all it took for her to get caught.

Now, he asks? She would love nothing more than for them to have more children. She had always wished Tony wouldn't be an only child. It would be foolish to have Rico start using a condom, but it was something she needed to think about. They had much to discuss. Why had he wanted her to have an abortion? And when he'd seen his son, his anger had been directed at her for keeping Tony a secret.

She sat in the bed and folded her hands on her lap over the sheet. "Yes, I know we have a lot to discuss." She looked into his eyes. "I have so many questions. We really haven't talked much."

Rico flung the sheet off, and in one motion, he was out of the bed. His hands on his hips, he was as glorious as one of the many naked statues throughout Palermo. He could have posed for Michelangelo. Rico's magnificent naked body made her mouth water.

"Perhaps we should dress for this discussion as you feel

that we have too much sex." His voice thundered through the room, then he turned and stormed out of the bedroom and into the bathroom.

Liz had no idea why he'd just gotten so angry with her. He was the one who'd told her to leave and then sent his Aunt Angela to meet her with an envelope full of money.

Ricardo clenched his fists and growled. Why did he let her get to him? He turned on the shower. *Liz is doing this because she does not want to be with me.* After all, she had left him first. She had gone out of her way to wait until he was on a business trip. *She knew he couldn't take her with him.* Liz had packed her meager belongings and walked out of his life.

He shampooed his hair and scrubbed his scalp in frustration. He *had* to calm himself—there must be something he missed. Liz would rather live in poverty than become his wife. He had to threaten her with custody of their son before she'd agreed to marry him. In bed, she was wild, last night in front of the mirror… the corners of his mouth raised. She couldn't fake her desire.

The hot water beat on his shoulders, relieving the tension. His mind combed over the past few days. They knew the photos weren't of Liz. He knocked the heel of his hand against his temple. The photos! How stupid was he? He shut the shower off and reached for a towel. She'd said there was only him. That night when he'd arrived home to find her gone, there had been a snapshot of her and Andre at dinner.

He ran into the bedroom. Liz wasn't there. He checked the dressing room, not there. He cursed, *"Maledisione, merda,"* and threw his towel onto the floor. Reaching for a pair of jeans, he then grabbed the first shirt his hand touched and stuck his feet into his loafers.

He had to find Liz before she did something stupid, like take Tony and run away. Would she do that? Yes, probably in her present mood. She was angry with him, not nearly as irritated as he was with himself. He had to find her and then call Massimo. He flew down the steps to Tony's bedroom. Tony wasn't there. Rico wondered how long he'd been in the shower. How much of a head start did Liz have? He reached for his cell phone as he ran down the main stairs. He jumped down the last four marble steps without looking in the living room and ran directly toward the back of the house and the kitchen. He stopped. Put his phone back into his pocket. There in the palazzo's bright and airy kitchen—not the breakfast room—Liz, Tony, and Anna sat at the granite-topped table, laughing at a joke Tony made. Their breakfast, slices of cheese, fruit, and fresh-baked rolls, for the adults, and an egg for Tony, were served on the palazzo's finest china.

Liz reached for Tony's glass of milk, helping him place it back on the table. He turned in his chair and slid off, running right into his father's outstretched arms. "Papa, you're home. Can you take me to see my pony today?"

"We will have to ask your mother and see what she thinks," Rico said.

"P-l-e-a-s-e, Mama, Please."

"Come and finish your breakfast, *then* Mama would like to talk with Daddy," Liz said in a firm voice.

"*Si amore*, we have much to discuss." Rico sat at the table, and Rosaria brought him a roll and a cup of espresso.

Anna sipped her coffee, and Tony ate his breakfast.

~

LIZ TENSED. *He has some nerve calling me love. He doesn't even know the meaning of the word. Oh, but if I have anything to say about it, he's going to learn. I'll teach him what love means.* Then she would pack her bags and take her son… and what? Not allow Tony to see his father anymore? Her shoulders slumped. She wouldn't do that to Tony. She remembered the look on Rico's face when he came running into the kitchen. He had looked frightened. It was an expression she had never seen on her proud Sicilian's face, and it told her plenty. When he saw them sitting at the table, she saw how he had instantly relaxed and almost smiled at them.

Liz, on the other hand, was still angry with the big, handsome jerk. He had on jeans, a button-down shirt, and Italian leather loafers. His hair was still damp from his shower… He had looked glorious in his earlier rage. Standing naked, his erection… magnificent. Those abdominal muscles of his well-defined and when he had turned—if she hadn't been so confused—she would have loved to touch the marble hardness on his butt. She couldn't understand why he had gotten so angry.

She wanted to have a genuine and trusting marriage with him. Raise a family. But a part of her held back, needing to keep herself safe. The pain of living without him flooded her, and it was difficult to turn her concerns off. She couldn't get hurt again. He called her *amore*, love in Italian, but he never said the words in English.

They did have to clear the air. Liz wouldn't live walking on eggshells, worried Ricardo would explode again over whatever he believed to be the slightest infraction—she didn't even know what had caused him to get so angry with her this morning.

Rico walked over to the sideboard and poured himself a second cup of espresso. Rosaria had gone to the laundry room. Anna looked at Liz, then she turned to Tony. "Would you like to go to the park? I push you on the swings."

"Okay."

He slid out of his chair before Anna could help him and scooted to Liz. Tony gave her a kiss. "You obey Anna. Hold her hand when you cross the street."

Tony smiled and nodded to Liz, then he kissed Rico.

When Tony and Anna left, Rico said, "We have to talk."

"Yes, we *certainly* do."

"Let us get out of this house. We will go for a drive."

She hoped he didn't mean to a river someplace and be done with her. "Is it wise to leave Tony?"

"He will be safe. We need privacy. There is much I have to ask you. Bring a light jacket, it may be chilly out." He grinned at her. "Nothing like New York winters, *Amore*, but Sicily can get some cold weather." He took his black Lamborghini out of the garage, lowered the top, and drove them to the foothills on the outskirts of Palermo and into the mountains, up winding roads with scissor-sharp turns.

He pulled over at a clearing on the side of the road, where they could park and look out at the city below. The view was magnificent—the blue water of the Mediterranean in the distance, ferries crossing to and from Rome, Naples, and even Genoa. The port was busy. Above, a plane made its approach to the airport.

Rico ran his fingers through his black hair and turned to her, "I need to ask you a question… When did you decide to leave me?"

Her head snapped around. "What?" She stared at him in astonishment. "What do you mean?"

"Do not play games with me."

Her voice rose, "Please. I, above anyone else, know this is not a game. Be more specific."

"You know what I am talking about. Do not be coy with me. When I came home from my business trip, you were gone. You left me that preposterous note and a photo of you and Andre at dinner."

Her anger took over. For the first time, she allowed her emotions to erupt to the surface. She vented all the feelings she had kept bottled up. "Look, I have no idea what you are talking about. Angela told me that you wanted me out of your home."

"What?" He shook his head.

Liz folded her arms across her chest, clenched her teeth and gazed at the city without really seeing anything. "You were the one who wanted me out. You met someone, and you took her away on your…" Liz lifted her hands and did imaginary quotation marks with her fingers. "Business trip. That's why you didn't want me to go with you. You had plans. Angela rushed me out of your home." She shook her head and shrugged. "It… didn't matter. I didn't have much and would only take the small amount of clothes I came with. I wanted *nothing* of the clothes you bought me." She swept the air in front of her with her hand. "Nothing." Liz adjusted herself in her seat and squared her shoulders before peeking over at him. "To have your aunt do your dirty work, to have her be the one to tell me… you took the coward's way out. What did you think I would do— cause a scene? That I would cry and beg you to keep me?"

Ricardo turned to her, his brows drawn, his lips pressed together. "We are getting off course." He lowered his voice, questioning, "Angela told you?"

"Yes, Rico, she did, then she proceeded to rush me out of the apartment. I left your note on the dressing table. You *know* all this. Why—"

Surprise etched his face. "I left you a note? What did it say?"

Her voice was low and flat with hurt. "Just the usual that such a note would say."

His surprise was replaced by anger. "Do not be modest," he said. "Tell me."

She shrugged. "You thanked me for all I had given you. You were never one to be tied down to one woman, and you were moving on with someone else, so please go and by the way, thanks for the great sex, but it was over." She sniffed and cocked her head to the side and tried to make light of it. "It was a dismissal without references. I felt dirty and couldn't wait to get out of your home."

His hands gripped the steering wheel, his knuckles white, his jaw clenched so tight, Liz thought it may break. He made a sound that came from deep in his chest as he turned to look at her. The fire in his black eyes made her shift away toward the car door and burrow into the leather seat of the Lamborghini.

"Let me tell you what I came home to," he thundered. "I came home to find Angela wringing her hands, all nervous. She said that you had decided I wasn't good enough for you. You wanted adventure and a different kind of man. One who didn't always work. Angela went on to show me a photo of you and Andre having dinner on *my* ship. She told me that she was the one who prevented you from taking the clothes I had bought you, as well as stopping you from taking the jewelry. As if I cared what you took. You were the only woman I had ever invited to live in my home."

Liz wasn't as quick as Ricardo in digesting what that all

meant. She studied him—he was in a rage but thank God it wasn't directed at her.

"Angela? But why? What purpose would our separation serve?"

"That is a question I am going to ask my dear aunt before I wring her neck." He started the engine.

Liz's brain began to work again. She stopped him with a hand on his forearm, his muscles so powerful under her palm, but she had to tell him the rest. "Ricardo, wait. Turn the car off there is... more you need to know," she whispered.

"More? Tell me all." The timber of his voice vibrated through her body.

"I was devastated and had no place to go." Liz didn't mention the night on the park bench or the women's shelter. "I didn't realize I was pregnant for quite a few weeks. When I did, I called you. Angela said you were away and had moved your new mistress into your home and your life. That you didn't want to be bothered by me. She was so consoling on the phone. She guessed I was pregnant. I told her, yes, I was, and felt you had a right to know." Liz watched the vein in Rico's temple pound, his face a red mask of rage. She became frightened for him.

His voice sounded calm, but she knew he wasn't. "Tell me the rest, Liz."

"I called again, and we made an appointment to meet. Angela told me that you didn't want to see me, but she would tell you of my circumstances. The next day, we met at a cafe downtown." Liz rested her head against the seat back. "Angela had been so consoling to me. She couldn't understand your reaction to the baby. She took out an envelope stuffed with money." Liz shook her head and closed her eyes to compose herself. All the feelings of rejection flooded back into her.

Rico enfolded her hand in his. "It is okay. Come on, you can tell me."

She looked at him. "Well, Angela handed me the envelope and told me that there was enough money for me to have an abortion."

At the word, Rico froze, his eyes blazed and then he did something Liz had never seen before. He made a fist with one hand and bit it. Beyond anger, beyond fury. His red face turned almost purple. A strangled growl came from deep in his chest. Teeth clenched, he snarled, "Please continue."

"Angela said… you didn't want my child… and you never wanted to be involved with me again. She told me to take the money and get rid of the baby." Liz shook her head, her voice quivered, and she brushed a tear from her cheek. "Rico, I couldn't. I could never do that, so I left the money on the table and walked away. When I was six months pregnant, I… met Anna, and she took me in."

He stared out the car window and cursed in Italian. "You know I would never ask you to do such a terrible thing. I am glad you are not of that nature either. I am going to get to the bottom of this. Why has Angela done this? I am going to take you home." He paused and kissed her hand. "You, Tony, and Anna will stay at the palazzo while I talk to my cousin Giorgio."

Liz sucked in a sharp breath. "Do you think Giorgio is involved?"

She had met Giorgio for the first time the other night, and he seemed quite friendly and happy that Ricardo was married and even had a son. She believed him to be honest in his happiness for Ricardo. Liz was no longer sure of anything. She had believed Angela, and now it looked as if, for whatever reason, she'd manipulated Liz to leave Rico. They had wasted all those years when they could have been together.

She wouldn't think of that now—they had to find out what the motive was for the things Angela had done.

"Rico, what else is your aunt capable of? Are you sure it will be safe for us to stay at the palazzo?"

"*Si, amore mio.* Yes, my love. I will call Massimo and have him increase security. You, Anna, and Tony will not go out while I am not home. Understood?"

She did understand but was worried, nonetheless. "What do you think her reason for this was?"

RICO TURNED TO HER, his arm going around her shoulders, and brushed a kiss on her temple. "Well, she went to a lot of trouble—she had to find someone who resembled you enough to pass for you." He smirked. "Too bad she didn't know that your beautiful body is not marred by a birthmark. She had to find Andre or whatever his name really is and arrange for him to be on the ship. It had to be a setup. She had to stage the photoshoot. Her reason for wanting us apart and keeping us apart is beyond my understanding. I will get to the bottom of this, have no doubt." He turned the ignition and shifted the car into gear.

The tires of his expensive sports car shot gravel behind it as he sped onto the road, taking the scissor-sharp curves down the mountain to the outskirts of Palermo. While driving, Rico had called Massimo about the extra security and to find Anna and Tony at the park. They reached the palazzo in record time. He left them at home.

AS HE DROVE toward his cousin's vineyard, his thoughts went back to six years ago when his father Giuseppe had a meeting with Ricardo, Gianni, and Giorgio. *He wanted the three of them to jointly run the company. Giorgio had voiced his opinion first. He didn't want the responsibility, nor the headaches. He was happy with the vineyards and perhaps expanding that portion of the business. He was content. Giuseppe understood how his nephew felt, so he agreed to the plan. Giorgio would become the president of Lombardo Wines, a subsidiary of DiMarco Enterprises. He would have a seat on the board of directors.*

Gianni, an up-and-coming attorney, wanted to handle all the corporate and legal issues for DiMarco Enterprises. They all knew there was only one man in the room to take charge and run the big company. That man was Ricardo, and he would become the CEO. Ricardo had built the shipping and cruise line for DiMarco Enterprises by himself. They now had seven cruise ships, and Ricardo had plans for two more this year and one each additional year for the next several years. Cruising had become big business, and he would make sure that DiMarco Enterprises had a giant share of the industry. Both of those businesses were a handful.

Ricardo arrived at his cousin's villa. A sprawling three-story stone structure covered in bougainvillea. On either side of the main building, two-story wings jutted out. The vineyards separated Ricardo's villa from his cousin's. Giorgio's work truck was parked in the circular cobblestone driveway, so Ricardo parked by it. He went up the weathered stone and brick steps and rang the bell. Giorgio, dressed in jeans, shirt, and lace-up work boots, answered the door.

"Hey bro. What's up?" He spoke in slang American, making Ricardo roll his eyes. It was all in fun, but Ricardo was too serious today, and Giorgio must have realized that because he switched to their native Sicilian dialect. "What's wrong? I haven't seen you this upset or serious in a long time. Come in."

Ricardo sat and accepted the drinks Giorgio poured for them. "Is your mother here? I know what I am about to tell you may be difficult for you to believe, but I have to tell you what she has done."

Giorgio stood and ran his fingers through his hair, "*Disgratzia*, what now? I don't understand her. She is always causing trouble... recently... I thought she was better. Settled, happy."

"She is back to her old tricks. This time is the worst. You remember how she wanted to come to New York and stay with me? We thought it would be the best thing for her to get away from Palermo, but now I know she had an ulterior motive." By the time Ricardo finished his story, Giorgio couldn't hide his anger.

"I haven't seen my mother since the night of the party, but I know where she is. She's in Palermo at her townhome."

Giorgio stood and paced from one end of the room to the other, then he turned to Ricardo. "Why would she do this terrible thing? To keep you from the woman you love and to deny you your son. I don't understand her at times." He shook his head, muttering in Sicilian, then he came to Ricardo and continued to pace back and forth. "I will confront her on this today. She has caused enough trouble for one lifetime!"

"I want to know her reason for this, but I will wait for you to talk to her. Then she will have to talk to me." Ricardo stood and looked directly into his cousin's eyes, "I know she is a handful, and all your problems with her since your father died. How she wouldn't even let your grandmother see her son on his death bed, the way she moved you away from this home because she hated it here, but you have to make her understand." Rico prepared to leave and said, "I am cutting her off without a penny of the DiMarco Enterprises money. No more monthly allowance—she has her own money she can live on. I will tell her when you finish talking to her." Ricardo hugged his cousin and left.

He knew his cousin was a good man and had been embarrassed many, many times by his overbearing mother. Now, Angela had completely overstepped her limits. Ricardo drove to his parents' home.

CHAPTER 14

The palazzo was quiet when Ricardo arrived home later that night. Several of the exterior lights were on and one by the garage entrance.

He climbed the back staircase, checked on his son, then walked up the steps to the master suite and into the bedroom. Liz read a book in bed, waiting for him. She smiled and closed the book, placing it on the bedside table. Liz's heart-shaped face, with her pert little nose and luscious lips, the mass of red hair flowing in waves around her shoulders, so beautiful—his wife. God, what he had put her through, and yet she was here for him.

He'd had her fired from her employment, threatened to take their son, and he'd made her beg him to keep Tony. The worst of all was that he'd forced her to marry him—he'd given her no choice in the matter.

Ricardo knew that Liz had done it all for Tony. But could she love him? He couldn't live without her. Rico needed her as much as he needed air to breathe. What would he do if she left him? If she took their son and went back to New York, he would be the one on his knees begging her to stay.

He'd never actually told her that he loved her in a language she understood or how much she meant to him, but he would. First, he had to tell her of all the hatred his aunt felt for him and why she'd done such awful deeds. He couldn't understand her reasoning, how she blamed him because Giorgio wanted to work with the land and not wear a suit and tie each day. His aunt had almost succeeded with her malicious plan.

Had he not gone shopping with Sofia, he would never have seen Liz or discovered that he had a son. His son, how Liz had taken care of him, protected him, never letting anything happen to him. He realized that she'd denied herself necessities and even food—she went without so that Tony could have the best in life. She'd kept him and loved him even though she thought the worst of his father.

He wasn't sure she could ever forgive him for how he'd treated her, forcing his will on her. He wouldn't be able to go on without Liz in his life. Was he brave enough to give her a choice to stay with him, or return to New York? He loved her more than he realized possible. All he wanted was to make her happy, protect her from people like his aunt. He hoped she would forgive him.

Sitting up in bed, she rested on the pillows, leaning against the massive wood-carved headboard, her hair cascading around her and curled around her breasts. The white nightgown she wore with a lace bodice and satin panels draped over her legs. The bedside lamp cast a yellow glow around the room as if lit by candlelight. Was it his imagination? The lace covering her breasts looked see-through—enticing his hands and mouth—her nipples extended under his gaze.

"You're so late... I began to worry. You sent me that text hours ago. How did the meeting turn out? What happened?" Liz sat forward, and the lace tightened over her bosom.

He couldn't think past wanting her. He needed her.

"Rico, are you all right?"

He mentally shook himself and lifted his gaze to her face, away from the temptation of her breasts. "*Si.* Yes, I am good."

She folded her hands in her lap, leaning toward him. "Please tell me."

"Angela will never bother us again. Giorgio will deal with her from now on." He slowly made his way to her side. "I do not want to think about her right now." His arms went around her waist as he pulled Liz up onto her knees. He bent and found her lips, open and ready for his kiss. Her satin-smooth arms looped around his neck, and her fingers massaged the nape of his neck, in a way that drove him crazy. He held her close as she arched into him.

He wanted to wipe out the memory of his aunt's cruelty. His beautiful, sexy wife had the power to help him forget. He cupped her head in one hand while his lips covered her softer ones, and his tongue devoured her mouth. He wondered if she could ever forget his behavior toward her when he'd first found her again. He would do everything in his power to make up for his overbearing and forceful actions.

His other hand roamed down to her breast. He stroked the hard nipple against his palm with the pad of his thumb over the lace.

She pushed herself into his hand. His Liz was eager for him. The pressure of his lips relaxed on her sensuous mouth, now more of a caressing motion back and forth across her soft, sumptuous lips. His hand slid along her back to the curve of her tiny waist sliding further to her buttock, massaging one lovely globe through the satin of her gown. Her mewling sound made him pull away before he lost control and tumbled her backward onto the bed, wanting to bury himself in her heat. He knew she deserved better than that.

Rico pulled away. He saw the confusion in her emerald-green eyes. "Let me go shave; my beard will scratch your delicate skin."

She touched his cheek, scraping her thumbnail along his jaw. "No. Rico, it's sexy. I like it."

He groaned and pulled her toward him. She went willingly as he bent down, and he saw her in the soft light. Yes, the top of her nightgown was sheer through the lace. The side panels of the gown were open from the waist, exposing the ivory skin of her well-rounded hips and shapely upper thighs. He had to sample the satin texture of one hip with his lips.

Rico knew that Liz wanted him as much as he wanted her as she pulled him close until he stood before her. She unbuttoned his shirt and ran her hands over his chest. He bent his head and took her soft and inviting lips. She reached his waist and unhooked his belt buckle. The rasp of his zipper filled the silence. Her small hands glided over his skin, reaching his buttocks. He felt the slight squeeze of her fingers.

So, she wanted to play? Well, he would let her, but he would play too. He lifted her nightgown over her head and completely exposed the luscious curves to his view. Bending to her mouth again, his tongue touched her full bottom lip. She moved, inviting him into her mouth.

His hands stroked down her back, fingers massaged her spine, reaching her buttocks, he said, "*Abraciame*. Put your arms around my neck. Spread your knees."

Rico's sexy low voice filled her with desire, and Liz did as he asked, bringing her sensitive breasts against his massive torso. Her nipples tightened and extended as they brushed the mat of his black chest hair.

She looked into his eyes and melted at the love she saw in the depths of his smoldering gaze. He leaned forward, his big hands on her buttocks. Rico bent her backward onto the bed. Her feet were at the edge of the mattress on either side of his magnificent body. Rico slid his tongue in her mouth to tangle with hers. He kissed her jaw and then her neck, trailing fire down her body. He kissed the underside of her breast and then sucked her nipple into his mouth. He treated the other to the same exquisite pleasure. His brand of loving filled her core with liquid heat.

She moved to hold him. He brushed her hands to her side. By the time his lips reached her abdomen, she was wild with her desire for him.

Rico lifted his head. "Are you sure my beard is not too rough?"

"No, it's perfect," she practically purred.

He dropped to his knees, and she couldn't hold back the zing of anticipation. He caressed the softness of her inner thigh, first with his hand and then with the tip of his tongue —ever so gently running his beard along her sensitive skin. A smile lifted her lips. He kissed her inner thigh, sending fire to course through her center. Her bottom rose off the bed as she offered herself to him. His thumbs spread her seam. He rubbed his chin at the core of her desire. A burst of pleasure shot through her.

"Rico, oh please. Yes. That feels sooo good."

He did that one more time, then he circled the bud with his tongue, sliding his tongue into her core and back to suck on the bud. Another zap of pleasure brought Liz's bottom higher off the bed.

Rico spread her wider, thrusting his tongue into her. Moans of pleasure escaped her and filled the room. Her body arched—she was so close to climax.

He slowed his movements, taking his mouth away from her. She groaned. He kissed her inner thigh.

"Rico, oh Rico, no, don't stop," she panted. She gripped his hair with her fingers.

"Shh, *amore mio*, just for a moment. It will be better, wait and see."

He didn't want to make Liz suffer. He just knew how much better her climax would be when he began again. She whimpered as he held the two globes of her buttocks in his hands and ran his tongue along her inner thigh. She called his name, in a half-plea, half-moan.

He spread her, and his tongue sought out her sensitive bud, the tip lightly pressing on the bundle of nerves, moving from side to side, slipping down and into her center. He thrust his tongue into her heat. She tasted sweeter than honey.

Her fingers dug into his hair, pulling him closer. He thrust deeper, lifting her to his mouth, licking the walls of her core.

She climaxed.

He felt the endless spasms as he held her to his mouth. She was wild, withering, and arching, her legs wrapped around his head. He held her buttocks, massaging the firm globes. Her legs relaxed, and he heard her murmur, "Ah, so good." He sucked the sensitive bud into his mouth one more time.

She did scream then as more shudders shook her petite body.

Rico stood and removed the rest of his clothes. Liz lay before him, her legs dangling off the bed. Her luxurious hair spread around her like waves of fire. Her eyes closed, she looked luscious and satisfied. He lifted her and moved to the center of the bed.

Lids at half-mast, Liz opened her arms to him and sighed.

"Oh, Rico." She smiled as his eyes devoured her. He needed to be in her now. Moving over her, the tip of his erection at her entrance, he bent to kiss her lips, and in one sure thrust, he was completely buried in her tight, hot passage.

Her heat surrounded him. He wanted to stay buried in her and never let her go. He knew he was a coward, afraid to give her a choice. She may choose to leave him. He thought of all he had done to her. Ricardo pushed those thoughts out of his head and, looking into her eyes, he thrust into her snug heat. His wife, who he loved beyond all else.

She called his name and moved her body in that way she had that drove him on and on. He was ready and couldn't hold back any longer, then he felt her orgasm begin. Holding him, caressing him in her tight heat. He thrust once more and took them both over the edge, as he exploded into her, he whispered, "*Amore mio, ti amo.*" My love, I love you. He rolled onto his back, taking her with him. She lay on top of him, the silken strands of her blazing-red hair forming a tent around them. He took her lips in a gentle kiss, his hands caressing her back as she leaned her head on his chest, content to just lie in his arms.

The following morning when Liz woke, Ricardo was still in bed with his arms around her. She smiled as he pulled her closer, snuggling her neck as she stretched. He said with a trace of laughter, "We had best get out of bed now, or we will not today."

Liz did laugh then. "You haven't been around your son long enough to know that Tony will search us out if we don't go downstairs soon." She felt Ricardo stiffen at her careless words and looked at him. "Oh, Rico, I am so sorry. I didn't think when I said—"

"No, *cara mia*, it is not your fault. You are the innocent one in all of this. I just want to strangle my aunt and her vicious vendetta." He kissed the top of her head.

"Will you fill me in on the rest of the details? You didn't tell me why you came home so late."

"*Si, amore.* I had to go to my parents. I felt that I owed them an explanation as to why I have a three-year-old son they'd never met. When I told my father all that Angela did, I had to hold him back, and my mother was worried that he'd have another heart attack. We talked, and my father decided that Angela is to be banned from any further dealings with DiMarco Enterprises." Rico stroked Liz's arm.

"I'm sure he was furious with her."

"Yes, and you know she'd wanted to come to New York to live in my house and be a glorified housekeeper to get away from Palermo. Running my house seems to have been an excuse to cause more trouble. My father feels terrible for my cousin Giorgio. He's always suffered with her as his mother."

"Oh Rico, I'm so sorry."

"Now, we had best prepare for the day. You shower while I shave. If we shower together, our son will come looking for us." He wiggled his black brows at her. "We would do more than wash."

She smiled and went into the shower. Liz had a difficult time believing that one woman could be so vicious. To keep Tony from his father, how could Angela be so cruel? Liz just couldn't understand that. At times, she felt that Ricardo should have tried harder to confront her. Not just believe the photos he had received of her with other men. Why didn't he trust her enough or at least come search for her? Not just blindly believe his aunt.

Liz's heart was still encased in ice. The edges may have melted some, but she couldn't completely let go of her fear that at any moment, something else could send Rico over the edge, and he would once again force her away. A part of her was unable to fully trust him. Not the way she had when she was young and innocent.

CHAPTER 15

A week before Christmas, the morning sun shone brightly in the mild Sicilian weather. Liz came out of the breakfast room on the main floor of the grand palazzo, searching for Ricardo.

She found him in his study at his desk. The built-in wood bookcase behind him held not only books, but trophies too. One soccer trophy included a photo of a much younger Ricardo. Liz looked at the other trophies lining one of the shelves. There were polo trophies and ribbons from other sporting events.

Rico tapped his pointing finger on his cheek. An espresso cup at his side, his custom-made suit jacket hung over the back of his chair. Two folders laid open on his desk, and he held a sheaf of paper in one hand. Rico was so intent on what he was doing that he didn't even hear Liz come in to the office or sit down on one of the leather chairs across from his desk. She cleared her throat.

He glanced up.

She smiled. "You were so absorbed in what you were reading, I almost didn't want to bother you."

"No, *amore*, what can I do for you?"

Now she was unsure of how to begin this subject. "Well, I was wondering… I was, thinking… I mean, I know you said that you were having a saddle and riding outfit made for Tony, but with Christmas just around the corner…" Her voice trailed off, and she looked down at her hands folded in her lap. It was difficult to ask him for money. She searched for the words that wouldn't make her sound like a gold digger.

His eyebrows came together as he studied her. "Yes, I will be picking it up tomorrow." He read his papers again.

She cleared her throat once more.

Ricardo glanced at her with an expectant expression. "Is there something else you wish?"

In a tone so low that he probably had to strain to hear, she mumbled, "Well, yes, there is." She looked up at him. "How does it work… with gifts? Your family exchanges Christmas presents?"

"Of course, we do." He sounded indulgent and dismissive, as he went back to reading his papers.

Liz lost her courage and left his study. Walking back to their suite, she sat on the sofa in the sitting room and held back her tears. How could she tell him? She had no money of her own. Didn't he realize that she never even had the opportunity to cash her final paycheck? Liz wanted to buy him a present but with what money? What kind of marriage would this be? Now she felt cheap, dirty, the gold digger he had once accused her of being. The walls closed in, and she felt like a prisoner in his home.

All this time, had it only been sex for him? Beautiful Italian words without meaning. He'd told her he didn't need a prenuptial, that he would keep her satisfied. She knew she was easy, one look from those black-as-night eyes, one kiss from those sculpted lips, and she turned to putty in his hands. No matter what he said, or did, she always melted in his arms.

She hated his aunt and what Angela had done to them. More than that, Liz hated that Rico hadn't tried to find her and confront her when he thought she had left him.

She closed her eyes as despair settled into her soul—a feeling worse than all the years she had spent without him.

Liz walked down the stairs to the second floor. A smaller, cozy living room separated the six bedrooms, four of them guest rooms and one belonging to Anna and the other was Tony's bedroom. Anna sat on the comfy couch, busy crocheting. The chandelier in the middle of the coffered ceiling was on, and sunlight shining through the terrace door bathed the room. Anna looked up and patted the sofa. "Liz, come sit with me. Tell me what is wrong? I see your face."

"Nothing I want to talk about." She gave Anna a wobbly smile. "Tell me how things are progressing with you and Massimo?"

Anna's face was bright, and to Liz, she looked years younger. Putting her crocheting down in her lap, she took Liz's hand in hers. "You know... after my husband, I never dream I find anyone like him, but in just a few short weeks... well, Massimo is wonderful. We have so much in common, and I am happy for the first time in years."

Liz hugged her. "I am so glad for you."

Upstairs in his study, Ricardo was certain he had missed something important. He flipped through the pages of the original report from his private investigator, positive that his aunt was connected to Andre in some way. How and where did they meet? Angela had to have planned for him to be on the cruise. According to the report, Andre was French and owned several lucrative businesses.

Ricardo hunched over his desk, his elbows on the mahogany edge, with his hands under his chin. "What am I missing?" he muttered. "Where is the connection?"

He growled and threw the report to the side. Shoving his chair back, Rico stood and paced around the room. Deep in thought, he stopped short as he remembered something Andre had said one night at dinner. Such a little thing, but yes, that had to be it. Andre had mentioned that he loved Italian wine, especially wine from Northern Italy—the Emilia-Romagna region.

Ricardo knew his cousin Giorgio had planned on acquiring a winery in that area. DiMarco Enterprises did, in fact, purchase one for Lombardo Wines about five years ago.

"*There* is the connection," he said and hit his fist into the palm of his other hand.

His cunning aunt must have met Andre at that time and gotten him to help with her deceit. Rico grabbed his suit jacket and the envelope with the photos and ran out of the house without saying a word to anyone. He sped off toward his cousin's villa.

Rico had called Giorgio from his car. When he arrived, Giorgio met him at the front door. "Come in. Coffee?" They walked into the living room.

"No, thanks. Here." He handed Giorgio one of the photos. "Do you know him?"

A flash of humor crossed Giorgio's face as he held the picture. "Sure, that's Andre Bourbon." He looked at Rico with a quizzical expression. "How do you know him?"

Rico pushed his fingers through his hair before he told Giorgio what he suspected his mother had done. He gave Giorgio the photos to look at. "It's not Liz, but at first glance, you would never believe it wasn't her."

I'm speechless—I cannot believe my mother's actions. What is her reason for this malicious act?" He walked to the fireplace and leaned against the mantel. "I don't know where my mother is. She wasn't home when I went to talk to her. I've been making phone calls, searching for her. She's been avoiding me, but believe me, I'm going to find her and get to the bottom of this."

"While you see to your mother, I am going to fly to France and confront Andre," Ricardo said with a grim voice.

"Well… you probably won't have to fly that far. He owns a villa outside of Parma—that's where he is right now. I called, thinking my mother might be with him." He shook his head. "But she wasn't."

Rico hugged his cousin and said goodbye to him. As he drove back to Palermo, he called his pilot to have his jet ready for the short flight to the Parma airport. Thanks to Giorgio, Rico knew where to find Andre's villa. He knew that Giorgio would take charge of his mother and not allow her to cause any more trouble.

When Rico's plane landed, in Parma, a car and driver waited at the airport for him. They drove through Parma. The city housed one of the oldest universities in the world and was famous for its prosciutto, among other things.

Andre's butler answered the door to the villa—a sprawling one-story stone structure surrounded by mani-cured gardens. He directed Ricardo to wait in the foyer. Rico didn't have long to wait. He heard footsteps on the marble floor, and then Andre walked in. He was slightly taller than Ricardo with blond hair and silver-grey eyes. He stretched his hand out.

"Ricardo, what a surprise to see you."

"Do you know why Angela used you to set me up?" Rico asked bluntly.

Andre's brows came together, and his eyes became two slits. "I don't know what you are talking about."

Rico handed him a photo—the woman was on her knees,

and Andre's erection was in her mouth. Andre's face turned white, and he stumbled back. "What, impossible—" He stood straight and composed himself. "Where did you get this?" Andre stepped back and pushed his hair off his forehead with a shaky hand.

Interesting, so Andre didn't know he'd been photographed.

"Come into my office where we can talk." Andre led the way down the hall. "If you think you can blackmail me—"

"Blackmail? No. My aunt, the woman you know as Angela, used these to separate me from Liz."

"Angela? I can't say what her motive is. I'm not… aware… That woman in the photo approached me. We had sex. A one-night stand… That's all it was. I didn't know we were being photographed. It appears I was duped as well."

Andre went to the liquor cabinet in his office, grabbed a bottle, and poured a drink. He raised the glass to Rico. "Whiskey?" he said.

"No, *grazie.*"

Andre downed the liquid in one gulp, then poured another. "I'm sorry. I don't know more about the part I unknowingly played in your separation." He strode around his desk and came to an abrupt halt. "As we are speaking, I am beginning to put together some more of Angela's nasty plan. I have been made an unwilling pawn." Andre opened a file cabinet. "Rico, please sit. I have something for you."

Once again, Rico realized why his aunt wanted to come live with him in New York. *What a malicious bitch. How did I not see her betrayal? My own aunt, maledizone!*

ON THE FLIGHT back to Palermo, Rico had in his possession the proxy votes that were intended to take his company from him. Angela had used Andre so that he would be able to vote Rico out at the upcoming shareholders meeting. Rico couldn't believe the lengths his aunt had gone to. He couldn't understand why. Only Angela, in her twisted mind, knew the answer.

Andre would meet with Gianni the next day and discreetly sell the shares of stock back to DiMarco Enterprises. Ricardo had him sign the proxies to be safe. Anything could happen between now and tomorrow.

Rico knew that all would turn out well. Giorgio would have to keep his mother from causing more trouble. There would be no takeover bid. He had a son and a wife that he loved to no end. Life was good. He was anxious to get home to his family and for the first time in a long time, enjoy the holidays. He wanted to show Liz how magical Sicily at Christmas could be.

When he arrived home, he searched for Liz and finally found her sitting alone in the palazzo's formal living room, deep in thought. She jumped as his voice broke the silence. "Here you are." He sat next to her, put his arm around her shoulder, and pulled her toward him for a cuddle.

She didn't give into the hug. "Where were you? You have been gone most of the day." In a low, almost inaudible voice, she asked, "Why did you marry me?"

He leaned away. What was going on with her? He looked at Liz, and when she wouldn't meet his eyes, he gently put his hand to her chin and turned her face toward him.

"What do you mean?" he asked in surprise. "I married you to give our son a name. So that he would know his father." He tried to keep the anger from his voice but could not.

Ricardo knew that it was Angela's doing, but for some reason, he couldn't seem to get past Liz not trying harder to talk to him. To let him know she was going to have his baby.

He had to put that entirely behind him. They were together now, and he had his son. He hoped there would be more children. He wanted to see Liz's belly grow big with his child. The image made him hot and hard. Ricardo pulled her toward him, but she resisted, putting her hands to his chest, and pushed him away.

"Don't. Don't touch me." Her voice sounded tired. Lackluster.

"Liz, please talk to me."

Liz stood and kept her back to Ricardo. "I guess I knew that all along. You married me after you saw Tony, when Anna told you he was your son."

Rico rose and touched Liz's shoulder. She turned. He saw the anger flash in her green eyes. "I am very confused, Liz. I do not understand this. I married you—"

"Oh, so I should be thankful that you married me?" Liz put her hands on her hips. "Dragged me halfway around the world, away from all that I know. You keep me here." Her hand swooped from her hip to take in the room. "A prisoner in this house, in a land where I don't know the language. I have no money of my own. I can't even go out to buy *you* a Christmas gift. You threaten to take my son from me and… and…" a tear slid down her cheek, "turned me into your whore for my son's sake. I hate you." She yelled the last sentence at him as she turned and fled the room.

Rico stood there, his face turning to stone in his anger. He couldn't believe Liz or the words she said. Her words confused him. He ground his teeth in frustration. She had built a large head of steam and needed to cool down. Nothing could be accomplished with them both yelling. He shrugged a shoulder for she was entitled to her anger. He decided not to go in search of her. Let her calm down, and then he would try to reason with her. And never have to hear her acidic tongue turn on him again. His whore, indeed. *How could she think that?*

As he climbed the marble stairs, he heard Tony and Liz laughing while they played in Tony's room. Every day he saw what a good mother she was, how she cared for Tony. He admitted to himself that she'd been hurt the worst by his aunt. Ricardo continued up the stairs to his study. He opened his safe, taking out the package that Gianni had sent him a few days ago.

The thick bundle contained deeds to the properties he owned around the world, his bank statements, and stock certificates. All his personal wealth now bore both their names. Ricardo Antonio DiMarco and Elizabeth DiMarco were inscribed on each. He opened another envelope and looked at the credit cards he had ordered for Liz. He'd planned on giving her these documents for Christmas so she would see how serious he had been about no prenuptial. All his wealth belonged to her as well. He wanted a real marriage with her. He loved her. She *had* to know that. He proved it to her every time he took her to bed. He'd let her calm down.

Tonight, Massimo was coming to dinner. He and Anna had begun going out, and they'd struck up quite a friendship. Maybe an evening at home with friends would help Liz to relax.

That night, Liz came down to dinner with her fiery locks pinned up, hidden from his view. He recognized her designer dress from when she'd worked at the jewelry store. So, he thought, she wouldn't wear the clothes he bought her? No jewelry either... not *even* her wedding band or engagement ring. The battle lines were drawn.

She laughed with Tony, talked to Anna and Massimo, completely ignoring him.

Rico watched Liz from across the dinner table. *She is ready for war.* He was most definitely in the mood to give her exactly what she wanted. Practically telling him that he kept her against her will and using her. She could stay nude if she wouldn't wear the clothes he bought her... The part that really got to him was when she said she had no money of her own to buy him a Christmas gift. His heart twisted in his chest at that.

When it was Tony's bedtime, he wanted both his parents to bring him upstairs. Rico picked up Tony and carried him while Liz led the way.

Tony climbed into bed and asked his parents, "How will Santa know where I am? Will he find me? I was a good boy. Right, Mama?"

Ricardo ruffled his son's hair. "We will go buy a tree, Christmas lights, and decorations so that Santa can have a place to put your presents. That will be fun? *Si.*"

Tony's face lit up with excitement. "Yes, yes, when can we go?"

"*Domani.* Tomorrow after breakfast. You need to go to sleep now, okay?" Ricardo bent and kissed Tony on the cheek.

Liz kissed him next. "Sweet dreams, my darling."

She walked out of Tony's bedroom, closing the door behind her. Ricardo, waiting in the hall, smiled. Liz ignored him. She walked past him to rejoin their guests. He held her arm and spun her around to face him.

"I like this game you are playing."

She shivered.

Rico whispered into her ear, "Later, I will take the pins from your hair, strip you of that garment." He slid his hand under the dress, reaching her buttocks. "It will give me great pleasure to see your luscious body naked."

He was hard and pulled her closer so she could feel the bulge of his desire against her softness.

She pushed away. "No."

Anger and frustration battled in Rico. "No. No, Liz, do not pull away. Is this not what you expect? This is the way you feel I treat you." He bunched her dress up around her waist. "I could take you against this wall, satisfy myself—with no consideration for your pleasure—then we would go back downstairs to our guests."

She squirmed and tried to push him away from her. "Stop. Stop it," she hissed.

"What do you think? Shall I?" His hand brushed her tight curls.

"No," her panicked whisper reached his ear.

He moved one finger along her seam.

"No. Please," she almost sobbed.

He removed his hands from her body, smoothed the dress down around her shapely legs. He spoke in a hoarse whisper, "We have guests downstairs."

She led the way back to the living room. He had to control the anger that threatened to consume him. She was the last person he should be angry with. When he saw her left hand and her ring finger minus her wedding band, an emotion he'd never felt before gripped him. Fear. Fear of losing her again. He'd hated all those empty years without her.

ANNA AND MASSIMO were in the formal living room where Massimo had poured after dinner drinks. With a hand that trembled, Liz took the glass, and in a very uncharacteristic effort to calm herself, gulped down the dark-amber liquid. Her throat burned, and her stomach caught fire—her eyes welled with tears, and she began to cough.

Anna joined her with concern. "Liz, come sit down. What is wrong? You are not yourself tonight." Rico brought a glass of water over to Anna. She held it for Liz. "Here, drink this."

Liz felt better after the water, and the burning in her stomach became a warm glow. She wouldn't look at Rico, so shaken by what he'd done in the hall, right outside their son's bedroom. If he'd really wanted to take her against the wall, he could have—she didn't possess the strength to stop him. She had to get away from him. She just had to, but there was her son to worry about. She had no money—she didn't even know where her and Tony's passports were kept. All of this added to her misery.

Tony loved his father, and he'd adjusted so well to all the changes—she couldn't take him from Rico. She wouldn't be a martyr about this either. She and Rico would have to come to an agreement of sorts… Her head spun. She didn't drink on a regular basis, and the alcohol began to have an effect on her. Liz calmed down enough to sit on the couch with Anna. They chatted quietly, while Massimo and Rico stood near the bar, discussing business. After a while, Anna and Massimo excused themselves and left for the night.

CHAPTER 16

$\mathcal{R}$ico turned to Liz, one brow raised then both brows furrowed. He had such happy news to share with her. His company was no longer threatened by a hostile takeover. Andre had been a puppet in his aunt's game. Angela had been stopped in her efforts and wouldn't be a bother to them any longer.

Earlier, he had been surprised when she said she felt like a prisoner and a whore. He'd never wanted that. The part about not having money to buy him a Christmas present tore at his heart. He knew of only one way to reach her—carry her up to their bed and make passionate love to her all night long. Without a doubt in her present mood, and her ideas on why he'd married her, she would put up a fight. Maybe a good argument was what they both needed to clear the air and get this marriage on the right track.

With that thought in mind, his deep voice broke the silence, "Come. Let's go up to your prison cell." He scooped her up in his arms and headed for the stairs.

Liz kicked her legs and pushed at Rico's broad chest. She

used all her strength to force him to put her down, but she couldn't budge him.

"Put me down. I'm not going anywhere with you. Stop. I—"

"No, Liz."

His voice rumbled deep in his chest. "You listen to me. We will have this out once and for all."

On the second-floor landing, she tried again, "Put me down." He didn't answer her and continued up the steps in a measured way, not hurrying, as if she weighed nothing at all. He entered their bedroom and moved his arm from under her knees. Her legs slid down his body as he stood her in front of him.

He turned and locked the door. With purposeful, slow steps, he strode toward her, his face a mask of indifference. He reached her side, and his lips became a thin cynical line of determination. He grabbed for the zipper of her dress.

"No," she cried out. "Oh no. Stop it." She wouldn't allow him to mistreat her. Liz held his gaze, and he dropped his hands to his sides.

She took a step back, and another. One of his black brows shot up.

She stopped. "Don't—you will not force yourself on me— ever."

Rico stood so close, the scent of cologne and virile man made her dizzy, but she wouldn't back down.

"I never wanted you to feel as if you were a prisoner here. And certainly not an easy woman. I didn't realize how you felt. This is our home. Come with me to the sitting room, we will be more comfortable in there rather than standing in the middle of the bedroom."

He took her hand, and Liz pulled it away but followed him into the sitting room. "Please sit, so we can talk." Liz ignored him and stood by the sofa, not willing to sit down.

"No. You do not wish to sit? Okay, but we are going to talk."

She hoped her glare would cut through him. "I have nothing to say to you, and I don't want to hear anything you have to say. I'm your wife and yet your treatment of me is appalling. You never even apologized." She turned her head.

Rico's accent grew heavy, "Well, you will listen to me. You accuse me of keeping you against your will. That I forced you to marry me, and you say I treat you like a prisoner and use you. None of this is true." He paced in front of her, reminding Liz of an attorney arguing his case to the jury. He paused before her, taking her hands. "Maybe I did force you to marry me… was that such a bad thing? We have a son who needs both his mother and his father. What is wrong with that? I kept you here because I was trying to keep you, Tony, and yes, even Anna, safe from my aunt. I had no idea what she would do. What she is capable of."

Surprised, Liz raised her head. *His aunt duped me once, did Rico think she could do more harm? He was being protective.*

"Please sit with me," Rico said. "There is more."

Liz moved to the sofa and sat, curious to hear what Rico had to say.

"I'd rushed home so happy, wanting to share the great news with my wife, but what do I find? Her waspish tongue accusing me of all sorts of despicable things. I was keeping you safe." His voice rumbled around her. "I didn't realize my actions didn't show that. It is no excuse… I had so much on my mind, from before I saw you in the jewelry store. I'm under a deadline, although as I've said, that is no excuse for my behavior."

He stood and took a step toward the door, then pivoted and in a much softer tone said, "Please stay here. I was going to wait for Christmas… but well… just please wait. I have some things for you."

Liz stiffened and tossed her head. *His deadlines—he forced me to marry him—what do I care.*

He left the room, and she stood, took a step, and stopped. Where would she go? She decided to hear what he had to say and then... she'd let him know how things would be.

When Rico came back, he held two envelopes in his hand. He placed the smaller one on her lap. "Here, I would like you to have these. I ordered them when we married."

She looked down at the envelope and shook her head; she wouldn't touch it.

"Take it." It was a command.

Liz closed her eyes for a moment, pressed her lips together. "What, Rico, is in here, more photos? More lies that I have to defend myself against?"

"No, *cara mia*, please believe me... sometimes I scare myself... but no more misunderstandings."

Then she lifted the envelope, opened the flap, and peered in at credit cards. The first one was a black American Express card just like his. Her name, Elizabeth DiMarco, was boldly inscribed on the front of the card. There were other credit cards with her name on them. Behind those, cash—American currency as well as euros. She didn't know how much, but she could tell it was a significant amount.

She cocked her head to one side, looking at him. His face was devoid of the earlier rage, and his ebony eyes warmed as he held her gaze, a flame burning in their depths. Time and again, he proved to her that the old Rico was back, the one she'd met one night on a cruise to Bermuda and fallen in love with.

From behind his back, he brought out a gift box and offered it to her. "I bought you this. You will need a place to keep your money and plastic."

The famous Italian designer's double G's was printed on the lid. She lifted the top of the box—tissue paper rustled in her fingers as she parted it to reveal a rectangular wallet. She ran her hand along the leather and then turned to him. She raised a brow in question.

"I know you do not have a wallet. I saw this one the other day and had to get it for you."

Out of the larger envelope, he removed legal documents. "These are the deeds to all of the homes I own. They now have both our names on them."

Her eyes widened. *He'd meant us to have a real marriage from the beginning.* She didn't say anything.

"These are bank statements and stock certificates, all with both our names." He reached into the envelope and pulled out her and Tony's passports.

Her heart thudded.

"These, my passport, and more I keep in the safe in my study. I will show you where it is hidden. The combination shouldn't be difficult for you to remember." He paused, and his voice caressed her as he said, "It is your birth date."

Their eyes met. Liz was speechless at his words, but even more so by the tenderness for her on his face. He cared for her.

So why hadn't he searched for her? He'd never tried to confront her when he thought she'd left him for Andre.

Her jumbled thoughts were conflicted over his loving actions now, and yet Rico had just turned his back on her and gone on with his life, proving she'd meant nothing. He'd never fought for what they had. What if he turned his back on Tony and her again? She couldn't allow herself to trust him.

"What do you think, *cara mia?*

Liz wondered if she should confess her doubts to him. In the end, she realized that they needed to clear the air—she had to open herself up to him, even if he would see her vulnerability. She had to be strong if they would move past this.

Liz placed the wallet and envelope on the sofa next to her. She swallowed her pride, along with the lump in her throat.

Rico had taken the first step handing her his wealth, his homes. She searched his face. "Why did you never try to find me, confront me?" Her body tensed. "Why did you just accept that I wanted someone else, turning my back on all we had?" She lifted her bare feet onto the couch and hugged her knees to her. "I couldn't fake the love I had for you. You had to know."

She saw sadness in the depths of his dark eyes.

Sadness? Her frustration erupted. "For goodness sake, we made love just before you left on your trip. Do you think I could have done that knowing I was going to leave you?"

Tears welled, but she brushed them away.

"Ah, *amore mio* I'm sorry for my behavior toward you." He came off the sofa, Rico dropped to his knees in front of her, his voice thick with emotion. "I love you and have always loved you." He clutched his chest with both hands. "My heart was broken when I saw the pictures... I know it does not justify my actions."

The tenderness on his handsome face reached a place deep in her heart.

"It clouded my judgment. I didn't want any more pain. I knew I couldn't take more of the agony. If I saw you, in person, with another man's hands on you... it would have killed me. Everywhere I turned I saw the images of you and Andre... then the others."

She raised her head from where she'd rested it on her knees. "But—"

"Yes, now we know it wasn't you. Remember at the time I did not. I thought it was. I threw myself into my work. I had to escape. I left New York and traveled to Germany, England, even Australia for business. The thought of what I had lost—it was too much to bear. I never searched for you, because had I seen you and Andre together, I just do not know what I would have done."

His fingers reached to twine with hers as he pleaded, "Can you find it in your heart to forgive me for being so untrusting of you? You must understand how devastated I was when I saw the photos."

Rico had just opened his heart to her—but she needed a chance to digest his words. It was all overwhelming. Liz studied his handsome face, tempted to caress his strong jaw in comfort. Instead, she gave his fingers a squeeze and pulled her hand from his. "I need to be alone." She remembered her own devastation, the raw pain she'd felt when she thought of him with other women—but did that excuse his behavior?

"You take all the time you need. I am here for you, *amore*. Always."

Rico left her in the sitting room.

She stayed on the sofa and tried to come to terms with her feelings. The clock on the mantel chimed midnight, and still, she sat. Eventually, she rose, going into the dressing room for a nightgown. Rico lay in bed. She knew he was awake, but she didn't want to talk and certainly not make love with him. Her feelings were too raw.

She used her frustration like armor to keep him out. He had bared his soul to her, given her the room she needed to face a future with him, yet something caused her to hold back. Liz lay as close to the edge of the bed as she could without falling off. He moved to her side, but when he reached for her, she stiffened.

He must have felt it because he said, "I just want to hold you. More so, again I wish to apologize for my brutish behavior. I would never raise my hands in such a manner again. This is no excuse, but my frustration over my aunt has made me forget how innocent you are in all of this."

She relaxed, and he cuddled her back into his muscular body.

It took her a long time to fall asleep.

In the morning after breakfast, as Rico had promised Tony, they went in search of a Christmas tree and found just the right one. "We'll need all sorts of decorations. I've never had the desire to put up a tree. We will have to buy everything to make the palazzo special for the holidays."

She looked at Rico in surprise as he lifted the tree they'd picked out to tie onto the roof of the BMW. "You don't have any?"

"Christmas trees are new to Italy," he said. "Only in recent years have they become popular. The *Presepio*, the nativity, is what we usually celebrate around."

Liz fastened Tony into his car seat for the drive to the palazzo.

"When we get back home," Rico said as he maneuvered the car through Palermo's traffic, "pack an overnight bag for you and Tony. We will take a short trip to a Christmas market where we can purchase decorations and enjoy some of the local customs."

The short trip turned out to be to Rome on his private jet. They had lunch on the flight, and then he took Liz and Tony to the famous Piazza Navona's Christmas Market. The crisp air was full of wonderful aromas, like chestnuts roasting at a food stall, and other street food that smelled heavenly as they walked by.

Tony saw the large carousel in the center and wanted a ride on it. The market had all types of vendors selling hand-made ornaments and other decorative items from the many regions of Italy. Music played through the market, and there was more than one stall selling marionettes. Tony recognized Pinocchio, and Rico bought him one of the larger dolls.

"There is another holiday we celebrate called *La Befana*—it is the night the Christmas Witch brings presents to the good little boys and girls. We hang stockings by the fireplace, and she stuffs them with gifts." Rico stopped at a vendor to buy a smaller Pinocchio ornament and *La Befana* ornament for the tree at the palazzo. Rico carried Tony for a while. With their heads together, Liz marveled at how much Tony resembled his father. The same black hair and the same black eyes.

They passed by one stall with stockings to hang by the mantel. Tony picked out a special stocking for Anna. They had it embroidered with *Nonna* in gold letters.

It was dusk by the time they met their driver for the ride to the hotel. Rico ordered dinner to be sent up to their room —a very spacious luxury room with a king-size bed and a sitting area that included a sofa, coffee table, and two side chairs along with a large-screen TV hanging on the wall. The day had been fun filled for all and long for Tony. During dinner, he rubbed his eyes, reminding Liz that he had missed his nap time.

"Let's get ready for bed," Liz said. "You can have a bath and then tonight, you can sleep in the big bed with Daddy and me." Tony didn't argue but showed his excitement at sleeping with his parents by going right into the bathroom and reaching for his toothbrush. Liz turned on the tap for the tub, wondering what Rico would wear; the man always slept naked. Tony, fresh from his bath, climbed onto the bed that Rico had turned down. Tony fell asleep talking about Santa and the Christmas Witch.

Rico moved to the couch and turned on the TV. He watched the news, and Liz joined him.

He lifted his arm and put it around her shoulders,

nudging her closer to his side. She didn't understand one word of what was being said on the television, but the same had been true for most of the day.

She knew he would respect her wishes and not make love with her; she was positive that was the reason behind his choice of a hotel room and not a suite. He would give her time—today had been a good test. They had walked together in the piazza, holding hands. He told her about his childhood and his memories of Christmas. They'd laughed together, and he'd carried Tony while Liz had linked her arm through his.

She focused on the TV. "I think I will have to take Italian lessons."

His face showed his delight, and Rico brushed a kiss on her brow. "Yes. I will hire a tutor to come to the house and teach you. Our son seems to be learning the language quite well, but he can benefit from some small lessons too. We can speak English at home, so Tony does not forget, and we will talk Italian when we are out." He snuggled her closer to him, and she rested her head on his shoulder, breathing the scent of his cologne. "Let us see if we can find something in English to watch." He flipped the channels and found an old movie that was just beginning.

In the morning, they dressed and had breakfast in the hotel restaurant. Rico took them on a tour of Rome. The traffic was worse here than in Palermo, she would never be able to cross the street without Rico guiding her and Tony. Manhattan was tame and organized compared to Rome. They went to the Colosseum. Then to St. Peter's Square, where they admired the Christmas tree and the large nativity, along with many other tourists.

Rico said that this year, the nativity had been made from sand brought to the Vatican from an area near Venice. It was an exciting day. They bought more ornaments and then while walking around the street near the Vatican, shepherds called *Zampognari* came down the mountain playing bagpipes and flutes, dressed in traditional wool cloaks as they performed tunes in the piazzas. In the late afternoon, Rico, Liz, and Tony flew back to Palermo.

Anna waited for them at the palazzo. She'd gone out to buy some decorations as well. Now, the four of them would decorate the tree together.

Ricardo made a playlist of favorite American Christmas songs to listen to while they decorated. Liz suggested that he add the Italian version of Jingle Bells as well. Rico had also bought some animated children's Christmas movies for Tony to add to his DVD collection. Even the housekeeper Rosaria joined in the festivities, making hot chocolate. The aroma of her gingerbread cookies baking in the oven wafted through the house. Ornaments and garland glinted against the red, blue, green, and gold twinkling lights on the tree. Tony and Rico sat on the floor playing with the train set that Rico had surprised his son with. Liz sat on the sofa, watching them. Tony's excitement every time the whistle blew brought a smile to Liz's lips. She'd learn Italian, and Rico said he'd teach her how to drive a car so she could be independent.

That night, after all the decorations were up, and the tree lights twinkled on the tree, Tony had gone to sleep exhausted from all the fun they'd had.

Rico ached to make love to his beautiful, seductive wife, and he ached to be in her, thrusting deeply, taking them both over the edge into ecstasy. He knew she needed time, and he would give her all she required to not only come to terms with her new life, but the space to feel at ease in their relationship. He wanted her to come to him. Rico had been encouraged when she'd said she wanted to learn Italian.

He didn't want her to think that all he wanted was sex. He needed so much more, to always be with her. When he made love with Liz, it was more than sex. The lovemaking had an emotional connection that he'd never felt with anyone else. He wanted to make her happy and keep her safe.

THE DAYS LEADING up to Christmas were full of invitations to family gatherings. From the moment Rico had introduced her to his parents, Liz had been made to feel welcome and a part of the family. Sofia had recognized her from the jewelry store and though she didn't know the whole story, she'd been thrilled that her suggestion to go to that store had brought them together again.

Liz saw what a close family the DiMarcos were, and she knew how nice it would be for Tony to have the large family she never had. Gradually, she let go of the last bit of ice encasing her heart—though the fear of Rico hurting her again clung to the outer fringes of her mind.

She tried to come to terms with her true feelings for him. She had loved him at one time… now she wasn't sure if she could abandon her fears and let her feelings for him take over again. He had opened up to her the night he gave her those gifts. It showed her how committed he was to their marriage and to her.

She realized that although the anger had melted away, the memory of the pain she had lived with on a daily basis had been unbearable. She couldn't live like that again. Not a day or a moment had gone by that she hadn't thought of him, missed him. In fact, that very morning before he'd walked into the jewelry store, she had been thinking of him. Could she turn her back on the hurt and trust her husband to keep his promise that he loved her and would keep her safe? Liz brought her thoughts back to the present.

It was Christmas Eve morning and through the monitor, Liz heard Tony moving around in his room. She quietly slid out of bed and put on her red velvet robe and matching slippers. She turned off the monitor and tiptoed out of the bedroom, so as not to wake Rico. She went into her son's room. "Good morning, handsome."

Tony stood in his pajamas by his dresser. He had one drawer open and a pull-over shirt in his hand. "Mama, can we bake cookies for Santa?"

"Oh, yes. That will be so much fun. Let me help you get a pair of pants and your socks." When he was dressed, they walked out of his room and met Anna in the hall. "Nonna," Tony reached his arms up to her. "We are baking cookies for Santa."

Anna held him up for a kiss. "So much fun, can I help too?"

"Yeah," Tony sing-songed. "We're gonna bake cookies."

Anna and Liz both burst out laughing.

"Let's have breakfast, and then we can get started on the baking," Liz said, enjoying her son's excitement over Christmas.

IN THE EVENING, Rico, Tony, and Liz drove to Rico's parents' villa. She would have to start thinking of them as her mother-in-law and father-in-law. Rico had prepared her for the festivities. All the DiMarco family and their friends would be there. Anna and Massimo were also there. All *except* Angela—no one had seen or heard from her since she had disappeared the night of their wedding announcement. It had taken Liz awhile to realize Angela had tried once more to cause doubt between her and Rico.

They walked up the steps to the enormous villa. Liz wore a red Dior cocktail dress and silver and crystal high heels. Her long tresses were styled down around her shoulders, and her diamond earrings peeked through her hair. There was a chill in the air, and she wore a cashmere wrap to keep her warm. One day last week, her couture clothes and designer handbags appeared on her side of their walk-in closet. Rico had kept them for her. Even Tony's racer bed from their tiny apartment in Brooklyn had been set up in his room.

They walked into the drawing room where a Christmas tree stood to one side, decorated in festive gold and silver baubles. Rico and Liz greeted his parents. Tony kissed his *Nonno* and new *Nonna*. They said hello to all that were gathered. Children ran and played when one of Tony's little cousins saw him and raced to Tony. *"Giocamo?"*

Rico bent to his son and said, "He is asking you to play."

"Si. Play," Tony said, mixing both languages and running off with his cousin.

Rico had told Liz that tonight's meal would be all fish. The southern Italian tradition called *La Vigilia,* but she knew it as the feast of the seven fishes. There were two rows of tables covered in white linen and set with sterling silver, china, and crystal. There was even a children's table set nearby. The meal began with antipasti and ended with dessert and espresso. Uniformed staff served all. The festivities went on into the late evening, the excitement in the air as the children played and sang songs about Santa coming to town. Liz had changed Tony into his special Christmas pajamas before they left the party.

The moment Rico put him in his car seat, Tony fell asleep. Liz sat in the passenger seat next to Rico on the short drive home. As he lifted his son out of the car seat, church bells rang all through Palermo. It was Christmas. Rico turned to Liz. "Merry Christmas, *amore mio.*"

"Merry Christmas." She rose on her toes and kissed a sleeping Tony on his cheek, and then Rico. He brushed a kiss on her temple. She went up the steps ahead of them to pull the covers back on Tony's bed. After laying Tony in his bed, Liz and Rico went downstairs to put his gifts under the tree.

"Tomorrow will be a busy day. You know once Tony sees his new saddle and riding outfit, we will have to take him to ride his pony?" Rico chuckled.

"It will be a busy day. We are going to your parents' house for a big feast." She patted her stomach. "As if tonight's feast weren't grand enough. Anna and Massimo will be there too."

She rearranged one of the presents then stood back to admire the tree. "Before we left this evening, Tony put milk and cookies out for Santa." Liz smiled up at Rico. "You had better eat them, *Santa.*"

"I will, but first…"

In the glow of the twinkling lights, Rico stood behind Liz and put his arms around her waist, pulling her against his body. She sighed and leaned into him.

He bent his head and whispered near her ear, "*Amore,* do you know how much I need you?" His lips kissed down the column of her neck to her collarbone, grazing the beginning swell of her bosom above the bodice of her dress.

"Rico—"

"No words, *amore…* let me love you," he said, turning her in his arms. Her luscious pink lips invited his kiss. His mouth moved over hers, drinking in her sweetness. Liz reached her arms around his neck, and Rico's lips brushed her sweet mouth.

Her arms wrapped around his neck, she stood on her toes to fit fully into his rock-hard body. Her lips opened, inviting his tongue in to run along her teeth and then swirl and mate with hers.

Her fingers slid into his hair.

His only thought—that Liz wanted this.

Yes. For the first time since she'd came back into his life, Liz desired this fully without his having to coax and woo her. Her hands brushed along the front of his shirt. Earlier, he had removed his tie and opened the first two buttons of his shirt. Now she reached for a button and one by one, she unfastened the remaining.

He lifted her into his arms and headed up the stairs to their bedroom. He stood her near the bed as she pulled his shirt tails out of his waistband. He helped her, slipping his arms out of the sleeves and taking the shirt, he sailed it across the room to silently land on the floor.

His lips never left her sensuous mouth, as she slid her open palms down his chest. Then she leaned into him, her naked breasts rubbed against him, driving him crazy as only she could.

He was Michelangelo's David, the chiseled perfection of his body covered by warm flesh. She loved the feel of him. Slowly, she dropped to her knees as she gazed up into those black-as-night eyes and felt the desire burn into her. His scent filled her head. With steady fingers, she reached for the button of his pants—the rasp of the zipper sent a zing of excitement into her core. Their eyes met, and she slid his pants and underwear down his thick-muscled thighs.

He stepped out of them. His erection—so beautiful. She circled his rock-hard shaft, her fingers unable to fully close around him. She touched her tongue to the velvety soft tip and tasted him.

He stood perfectly still, and Liz ran her left hand up his muscled thighs as she opened her lips, eager to take the pulsing head into the warmth of her mouth. Her hand moved up and around his hip and on to his marble-hard buttock. Caressing his buttocks, she moved forward so that she could take more of his steely member.

She licked along the hard length of him and lingered on the velvet-soft head. She sucked as much as she could of his length into the recesses of her mouth, using her tongue to stroke the underside. His rough voice groaned, "Please, *amore mio*, it is too much." Her core pulsed.

His hands went to the side of her head, his fingers tangling in her hair to stop her. She moved her head up and down, keeping him in her mouth. She almost smiled when she heard his husky plea.

"Ah, ah, *amore*, the sweet torture of your mouth is driving me crazy." She watched his face, loving his reaction. Rico's hands moved in her hair, "It is too much. I want to come *with* you." He lifted her off her knees.

She looked into his eyes as he unzipped her dress, and it pooled on the floor. He groaned, "No bra." Her thigh-high stockings and thong were all that covered her.

His erection throbbed in painful need. He had to be in her. Bending to kiss her swollen pink lips, she tangled her fingers in his hair. He lifted her and moved her to the center of their bed. She shimmied out of the thong.

"Leave the stockings, *Tesoro*."

She smiled and lifted her arms to him.

Rico kneeled on the bed, and with one knee, nudged her legs apart. Her nipples were stiff, and he had to feel the texture with his tongue. First, he sucked one taut pink nipple into his mouth, snaking his hand over her abdomen. He felt her muscles tighten, sliding lower—one long finger running along her seam to seek out her center. The moisture drenching him, he sucked on the nipple while he thrust that knowing finger into her heat.

She moaned his name low in her throat, "Rico." Another moan, and then she whispered, "Oh Rico, make love to me."

"*Si, amore.*" He moved over her, and her small hand guided his throbbing erection to the entrance of her heat. He entered her that first tiny bit, but she wanted none of that as she wrapped her arms around his neck, lifting her legs to go around his hips. She pressed her breasts, the nipples wet from his loving, into the mat of hair on his chest.

He mentally smiled, thinking this was the Liz he remembered, eager and wanting all he had to give. Her hands moved down his back, then back up to his shoulders. She lifted her hips, meeting his thrusts. The silky strands of her hair rippled like fire on the pillow. Arching her hips, inviting him to thrust deeply, she met his every stroke. He raised himself and locked his elbows, sending himself further into her heat.

"Oh yes." Her hands moved to his waist and the small of his back, pressing him for more of his length. Rico moved his hand to grasp her ankle and guide her leg over his shoulder. Liz gasped in understanding, eagerly sliding her other leg up to his other shoulder. Her eyes smoldered deep in the green depths as she gazed into his. Rico thrust fully into her tight passage. He smiled down at his beautiful wife, staying deep in her moist heat, moving his hips slowly from side to side.

Her breath hitched. "Oh Rico, you feel so good." Words she hadn't said to him in a long time tumbled out of her. He pulled almost entirely out and then thrust deeply again. She pulsed around him. Her cheeks were flushed, and her green eyes were full of desire. Her silky hair spread across the pillow in waves of red fire. Her ankles dug into his shoulders —he looked into her eyes and one of his dark brows rose.

"Noooo," she half-moaned, half-groaned, knowing before time what he would do. He found her clit and used his thumb and forefinger to apply pressure and manipulate the bundle of nerves as he stayed buried deep in her heat.

A burst of pleasure shot through her core, and her feet dug into his shoulders, lifting her, sending him deeper if that were possible. He moved his finger on her flesh, pressing and releasing the pressure, rubbing her clit, making her wild with pleasure. She pulsed around him, pulling him into her body.

He groaned. "Oh, *amore*." He couldn't hold back any longer; the waves of her orgasm holding him, caressing him, a fireball of pure bliss exploded in him, and he poured himself into her.

Her legs slid down to be caught in the crook of his

elbows, and he gathered her against him while their breathing returned to normal.

A lock of his black hair had fallen over his damp brow, and she reached a trembling hand up to smooth it back, then she touched his cheek. "I love you, Rico… I always have. No matter how much I tried, I could never forget you. I want you and need only you. You have melted the ice around my heart."

"*Ti amo*," He said and looked into her eyes. "Tell me again."

She looped her arms tighter around his neck. "I love you, Rico.

Her eyes widened. He was hard in her once more. He kissed her lips.

"Yes, *amore.* I want you again. I love you.
****

Thank you for reading The Sicilian's Betrayal. I hope you enjoyed Liz and Ricardo's story.

The Winemaker's Seduction is the next book in the DiMarco Empire Series. Read Maddie and Giorgio's love story of how a deal for a vineyard leads to a deal in the bedroom.

WHERE TO FIND MY BOOKS

You can find my books at your favorite bookstore, retailer, or library 

Or, you can buy them directly from me at my website https:// CindyReddingAuthor.com

Or,

Cindy's Store https://payhip.com/CindyRedding

If you prefer, please scan this QR Code with your phone

ABOUT THE AUTHOR

USA TODAY Bestselling Author **Cindy Redding** fell in love with happily ever after when she read her first romance at age twelve. Since then, she has been hooked.

A native New Yorker, Cindy lived on the beach in South Florida and now she lives in Las Vegas, NV, with her husband, of thirty-five years whom she married on Valentine's Day. She has two daughters. Her eldest is named after a heroine in one of Cindy's favorite romances.

Inspired by her travels around the world and her love of Italy Cindy's, sizzling contemporary romance novels come to life with hot men and the strong-willed, independent women who they can't live without.

Escape into a world were happily ever after, lives.

When she's not writing, you can find her taking long walks in the desert or driving to Disneyland.

Escape into a world were happily ever after, lives.

ALSO BY CINDY REDDING

The DiMarco Empire Series
The Sicilian's Betrayal
The Winemaker's Seduction
The Frenchman's Revenge

Christmas
A Fake Date for Kate
The Christmas Present

The Royals
A Royal Temptation

My Store
www.CindyReddingAuthor.com

ACKNOWLEDGMENTS

I would like to thank Christopher Hawke and Traci Hall of Community Authors for their invaluable advice and encouragement. I will forever be grateful.

I would also like to thank the three lovely ladies in my critique group. You ladies have taught me so much.

I want to especially thank SJS Editorial Services for their quick and thorough read.